Nissa's Place

Also by A. LaFaye

Nissa's Place

A. LaFaye

milkweed
editions

© 1999, Text by Alexandria LaFaye
All rights reserved. Except for brief quotations in critical articles or reviews, no part of this book may be reproduced in any manner without prior written permission from the publisher: Milkweed Editions, 1011 Washington Avenue South, Suite 300, Minneapolis, Minnesota 55415.
(800) 520-6455
www.milkweed.org

Published 2010 by Milkweed Editions
Cover design by Brad Norr Design

Manufactured in East Peoria, Illinois, in April 2010 by Versa Press.

10 11 12 13 14 5 4 3 2 1

ISBN 978-1-57131-697-4

Please turn to the back of this book for a list of the sustaining funders of Milkweed Editions.

The Library of Congress has cataloged the previous edition as follows:

LaFaye, A.
    Nissa's place / A. LaFaye.
        p.   cm.
    Summary: Uncertain of where she really belongs, thirteen-year-old Nissa leaves her Louisiana home where she lives with her father and new stepmother and goes to stay with her eccentric mother in Chicago.
        ISBN 0-689-82610-9
    [1. Mothers and daughters—Fiction. 2. Fathers and daughters—Fiction. 3. Stepmothers—Fiction. 4. Self-perception—Fiction. 5. Louisiana—Fiction.]   I. Title

    PZ7.L1413Ni 1999
    [Fic]—dc21   99-12257

To Sheila
May you find your own place

Nissa's Place

Nissa's Place

Changes

Dragging my book bag down Quince Road on my way back from school, I couldn't help wondering what I might find once I got home. The things in our house were shifting under the hands of Papa's new wife, Lara. I'd go to bed knowing everything in the parlor was snug in its place, then come morning, I'd head downstairs only to discover that the room had changed identities while I slept.

Years ago, Mama'd draped the fireplace with dried ivy. The vines and soot-black hearth made it look like a deep, dark cave opening up into our house. But Lara painted the fireplace white, then covered the mantel with photographs of people I don't know, lacing ribbons between them like snakes.

Lara even dragged my favorite chair with the velvet like grape jelly to Mama's keeping room. Mama'd filled the room with all the things she had a mind to use someday. Mama thought she'd change an abandoned porcelain sink into a fountain, but hadn't quite figured out how to make the changeover happen. Below the windows, Mama'd planted a garden of paint cans, pallets, half-painted canvases, and brushes. In the back half of the room stood a tangle of broken pieces of furniture Mama had intended to repair when she had the time. All that was gone now—hauled off to the dump. Papa did mail the paints to Mama, but he let Lara drag all of Mama's other keeping treasures off to a hole in the ground.

Stepping into the house, I let the screen door close with a loud clap to let Lara know I was home. It didn't seem right to call to her the way I used to call Mama. I turned to drop my bag onto the table where Mama'd always kept a vase of fresh-cut roses, but an ugly piece of furniture now stood in that spot. Looking like a wooden throne gone awry, it had a seat under an oval mirror ringed by coat hooks. Who'd want to sit on a chair surrounded by hanging coats? It'd be like plopping yourself down in a closet. And what kind of welcome is a big, old whatever-it-was compared to a beautiful vase full of deep purple roses?

That woman wasn't going to take my house from me. Stomping up the stairs, I heard the scraping screech of furniture being dragged across the floor. Knowing it came from Mama's room, I ran right in there.

Lara was tugging away at Mama's bureau. I shouted, "Where are you dragging that off to?"

Startled, Lara stood up and tried to smile at me, but she knew I'd caught her in the act. Pacing the floor like a lawyer pleading a case, she said, "Nissa, it's like living with a ghost. Everywhere I look, I see your mother. It's like she follows me around, declaring the place hers." Turning like she expected to see Mama behind her, she added, "I need to make this house my home. Do you understand, Nissa?"

Lara sat in the window. Her hand shook as she rested it on her knee. It looked kind of naked without the gloves she used to wear when she was courting Papa.

I didn't answer, so Lara said, "Your mother's building her own life up North. We need to build ours here."

Her comment lit a fire in me. I was ready to spit flames. She made it sound like Mama's new life had nothing to do with me.

I feared Mama was better off without me so I tried to protect the things of hers that still remained. And if anything in that house reminded me of Mama, her murals did—the garden path leading out of the kitchen, the bookshelves she'd painted in Papa's study, and the dreamy night sky on my ceiling. Just a look at one of those paintings made me hear Mama's laughter in the creak of a door. For that instant, she was back in the house and the last two years just melted away.

Taking a deep breath, I said, "Don't so much as take a crooked look at one of Mama's murals or I'll throw all your pretty things out into the street!" I was going to slam the door to make my grand exit, but I backed right into Papa.

Breathing down into my hair, he asked, "What did you just say, Nissa?"

Papa had a way of making you relive your mistakes so you'd not only see the error of your ways, but feel guilty enough to shrink. I bowed my head.

"You've gone to threats now, have you?" Papa said, stepping to the side so he could look me in the face.

"I don't want her ruining Mama's murals."

"Fine," Papa nodded. "Truth be told, I don't either. But threatening Lara is no way to go about protecting them."

"Yes, Papa. Sorry, Lara." I couldn't look at Papa, but as I left, I caught a glimpse of Lara sitting in the window seat all hunched over like a scared child. What did she have to be afraid of? Everything she ever wanted had come raining down on her—a husband, a house, a daughter she didn't have to give birth to or raise. And I was stuck with a stepmother and a house I didn't recognize.

Walking down the hall, I recalled something my best friend Mary Carroll had told me at lunchtime. As we'd sat with our feet dangling in Sutton's Creek, she'd said, "Don't think the house is the only thing Lara will change. She'll want your pa to change, too."

I'd laughed at the thought. There wasn't a single force in nature that could make my papa change if he had a mind not to. My mama had the force of a hurricane inside her, but my papa just bent in her fury like a tall, old pine tree.

She'd start raging about how he didn't have enough sense to stay dry in a sandstorm for letting his boss, Mr. Hess, run his life and Papa'd just waited her out, calm enough to peel an orange. When Mama'd let out all her hot air, Papa'd tilt his head, then say, "Appreciate your thoughts, Heirah Rae, but as I see it, I'm doing just fine living my own life."

That was Papa all right—living life as he saw fit. He'd never change. Just like Mama's garden. No matter how much Lara pruned and weeded and picked flowers to bring into the house, she couldn't take Mama out of that soil.

Stepping into the garden, I longed for Mama, but all the longing in the world wouldn't bring Mama back. I was a fool to even entertain the notion. But it sure would've been easier if Mama had kept her promise to write as regular as spring rain. I got a letter almost every week when she first went up North, then the stream of letters slowed to a trickle, one coming my way each month or so. Now, it'd been close to three months since I'd heard from her. My thirteenth birthday was a stone's throw away and I hadn't heard word one from Mama since late January. Leave it to Mama. Promises were like clipped roses to her. They're all beautiful and fresh when you first cut them, then they slowly fade way. She's never had what it takes to plant a promise and keep it healthy. It was enough to make me hate her if I tried, but I promised myself I'd never do that and, unlike her, I always kept my word.

I got that trait from Papa. He's as trustworthy as a priest. Mary told me priests hardly even think about sinning, let alone do it. Papa was that type of man. Not that Mama was a damned sinner or anything. She broke a lot of the rules that no one wrote down, like a mother shall never leave her children. Why isn't that a commandment? There's one that says you can't steal from your neighbor, but there's nothing about raising your own children. Now that doesn't seem right at all. You can't take a pie out of your neighbor's window, but you can walk out on your daughter without so much as leaving a note. Where's the righteousness in that?

"Have you let out all of your steam, Neesay?" Papa asked as he stepped outside.

"Yes, Papa." I bowed my head.

He planted himself on the stoop and stretched his neck. He'd been helping the Minkies stock their shelves over at the mercantile across the street. Now that they were getting on in years, they were even more bitter than ever that they never had any children. They needed all the help they could get to run things. Papa was glad to help. It kept us well stocked in dry goods. And he even brought home some chocolate bars on occasion.

Sitting next to Papa, I said, "Looks like you could use a hot bath." Lara'd had a bathtub in the house she'd owned before she met Papa. The place had fancy city plumbing and everything. She didn't have to lug buckets into the bathroom to fill up the tub. For half a second, I caught myself thinking it'd be mighty nice to live in Lara's house out in the new part of town. The place was just sitting there empty, waiting for somebody to see the FOR SALE sign in the front yard and do something about it. Chances of that happening were slim what with the Depression on and people losing their houses to the bank and all. It seemed a shame to let that fancy place just rot, but there was no way I was leaving my house on top of everything else.

Papa said, "No, what I'd like is hot rain."

"Hot rain?"

"That's right." Papa closed his eyes and turned his face up to the sky. "Rain hot enough to make your muscles loosen up. Wouldn't that be fine? Steam would rise up from the ground like fog. You wouldn't even have to get undressed. With a bar of soap, you could clean your body and your clothes at the same time." He faced me, smiling—the shadow of a growing mustache stretching out over his lip.

Laughing, I shook my head. It was times like these that I knew why Papa'd married Mama in the first place. They had a mind that saw the world in a swirled up special way that made me glad they were mine. And I guess nothing I ever did would change that. Thank God.

Mirror Images

I woke to the sound of a shattering dish. My thoughts flew to Mama—a memory of a morning long ago when she decided to get rid of our old dishes. Like watching a picture show, I could see Mama standing over the sink, a cracked plate in each hand and a smile on her face. Not a joyful smile that fills you up with a laugh, but a quick and wild smile like a flame. She flung one plate at the wall, then shrieked. "Isn't that a sound, Nissa?" she said, turning to me. "Thunder filled with glass."

She closed her eyes and threw the second plate. To shield myself from the glass, I scrunched up my eyes and shrunk down. In the instant the plate hit the wall, I felt an odd kind of calm. Time took a rest and without fear I could hear the plate break. The crack and crumble sounded so much like the roll and rumble of a special kind of thunder. I smiled.

"She hears it!" Mama shouted. "My Nissa hears the thunder." She threw another plate. Dropping her hands to her sides, Mama said, "Well, now I have to clean it all up." As she started to sweep, Mama said, "You know, if I crush this up like sand so it isn't even rough enough to cut your skin, I could glue it onto something. It'd make a mighty fine covering." Turning a shard in her hand, I could tell by the figuring look in her eye that she was trying to find a way to pound that glass down to sand. And she did. Piling all the glass into a folded towel, she smashed it with a rock until it was a fine powder, then sprinkled it over a glue-painted wooden box. She gave it to Grandma Dee to keep her spools of thread in. Every time we go to visit her, I run my hands over that box and think of glass thunder.

But the broken glass that morning wasn't thunder. And it didn't turn to sand. A plate slipped out of Lara's hands as she was washing dishes. I saw her stooped over the shards as I came into the kitchen.

"I can't believe this, a fine dish like that, gone in a flash." Shaking her head, she picked up a piece of glass to dump it in a towel.

Sometimes Lara could be so ordinary, she made me ache for Mama. "Crush it up and use it to cover something."

"What?" Lara looked up at me, a strand of hair falling down to point at her eye. Her eyes looked blue that day, like her dress. Lara's eyes shifted from one color to another to match her clothes like a chameleon hiding in the jungle by changing the shade of his skin to match the leaves.

"When Mama broke a dish, she ground it up so she could glue the sand onto something else to pretty it up."

"Sounds dangerous." Lara went back to picking up shards. She thought everything Mama did was dangerous.

"Fine." I turned to go into the garden. "Waste it then."

"I'm not wasting it, Nissa," Lara told me. "It's broken so I'm throwing it out."

"So it can fill up some hole in the ground with all of Mama's other stuff?"

"Is that what this is about?" Lara stood up. "You're angry that I broke something of your mother's?" Without even waiting for me to say a word, she said, "It was an accident, Nissa."

Mama didn't care about the things themselves in a "that's mine" kind of way. She just didn't like things going to waste—like old dressers that could've been made into something new. "That isn't it, Lara. I just don't think you need to throw it out. We can use it."

"Someone will get cut on the broken glass."

"Fine." I stepped outside.

Sitting on the stoop, I watched a flower bow its head in a breeze. One time, I saw a flower doing such and said to Mama, "Wouldn't it be nice if flowers had a tinkle like a bell, so you could hear them sing in the wind?"

Mama smiled. Pulling at my braid, she said, "Isn't that the truth of God." Her eyes stared off into another place. I imagine it was a place of singing flowers. Then she said, "You know, I suppose that's why they have wind chimes. The chime carries the voice of the flowers. They just toss their voices up there." Mama raised her hand in the air right quick to act out the voices jumping into the air. "Like one of those ventriloquists who throws his voice into a dummy's mouth."

I leaned into Mama, laughing. "That's silly."

"Of course it is." Mama rubbed my head. "But it's fun to imagine, just the same."

Glancing up at the doorway, I caught an imaginary glimpse of a wind chime made of broken glass. I jumped up and ran into the kitchen just as Lara was tipping up the towel to shake it off in the waste bin. "Hold up!"

My return gave Lara a little jolt of surprise. "What?"

"I'm going to make a wind chime out of it."

"A wind chime?" Lara turned her head and looked at me

sidewise like a fish peering out from its bowl. She held that look for a minute, then said, "That might be pretty." She smiled. Now I knew Lara's figuring look.

Setting the towel onto the table, she checked the clock. "We have a good while before school starts. We should go to the mercantile for some nice ribbon to hang the pieces."

"All right." I nodded. I didn't really want to build the chimes with Lara, but the thought of telling her made me feel a bit queasy.

I love how footsteps sound in the mercantile. They've got ceilings that are taller than our school flagpole, so the echoes of footsteps have plenty of room to travel around. For a bit, you can imagine your footsteps just bounce right out the door and travel on down the road toward Sutton's Creek. I was daydreaming about footsteps when we first walked in, so I didn't see Mrs. Minkie and Mrs. Fisher over by the clothing counter.

Lara was looking at the spools of ribbon at the end of the fabric table, holding up one, then another as if she were examining fancy rocks she'd found in a creek bed. I hung back and ran my hands over the bolts of fabric. Sometimes Mama and I would go to the mercantile and make up stories from the fabric. Mama would say, "See this here green check, Lucy Mavel has a dress made out of this fabric. Well, it was her sister Tilly's really, so it's too long and Lucy's always tripping on the hem."

I'd add my bit, saying how Lucy never takes it off now that Tilly's gone off to study piano in Shreveport. I didn't know Shreveport from Dallas, Texas, but it sounded like a place you'd go to for studying piano.

"What are you doing, Nissa?" Lara asked.

"Dream-remembering. Mama always said memories are coated with dreams."

Lara smiled, then said, "Well, I've been standing here thinking about how much you look like your mother."

Mrs. Fisher said, in her buckboard-bumpy voice, "I think she looks like her father, the same deep-thinking eyes and straight hair." As Mrs. Fisher spoke, I could hear Mrs. Minkie mumbling beside her, saying, "I wouldn't be proud of having anything like that Mama of hers."

Sometimes, I wish I could just will things to happen. Like having Mama in that store with me. She'd know just what to say. I remember how she'd leave people with their mouths hanging open wider than a barn door on a windy day. Me, I couldn't think of two words to put together to get back at crabby old Mrs. Minkie and her nodding friend, who obviously agreed with her.

Lara picked up a spool of navy blue ribbon, then brought it over to Mrs. Minkie like nothing had happened. "I'll take a yard of this ribbon, Miss Agnes."

"All right." Mrs. Minkie grabbed a yardstick down off the shelf behind her to measure the ribbon. Mrs. Fisher kept her eye on me like she expected me to do something just awful if she turned away. Made me wonder if she could hear my thoughts.

"Tell me, Miss Agnes, did you ever finish that painting of your garden you've been working on for so long?"

"Oh, heavens no." Mrs. Minkie laughed her crinkled-newspaper laugh. "I gave that up years ago."

"Well," Lara smiled, and I saw a flicker of a flame in her eye. I'd seen revenge before and knew it on sight, so I was smiling too when she said, "My. Then you should come over to the house and see the beautiful painting of a garden Heirah Rae put on the kitchen wall. It looks so real, sometimes I think I can just walk right in and pick me a bouquet."

"A painting on the wall? What on earth for?" Mrs. Fisher

made it sound like Mama had built a trapeze in our house or something.

But Mrs. Minkie looked punched, her face all sunken in and angry. Lara had sent it home. I had all I could do to keep from laughing. Cutting the ribbon a few inches short of a yard, Mrs. Minkie said in a voice about as sweet as arsenic, "I bet it's just lovely."

As we walked out of the store, Lara said, "She even took painting lessons so she could finish the painting."

"Mama never had a painting lesson in her life," I told Lara.

"I know." Looking over her shoulder, Lara added, "Those two could take a few lessons on how to treat people right."

As we sat out in the garden, picking just the right pieces for the chime, I noticed how Lara's hair kind of curled up at the ends when she let it down. She was humming a wispy tune and turning the pieces this way and that to see how they'd look in the wind. A funny kind of feeling came over me. For a moment, I caught a reflection of Mama sitting there. Like the mirror image in a lake. It was her, but not her. Lara and Mama shared things I never noticed before. That gave me a little peace.

Counting Stars

I used to wish days would fly by faster than a bird heading south with a hurricane on its tail, but the closer it got to my birthday, the more I prayed time would stand still. Afraid that the day would pass and I wouldn't hear from Mama, I didn't want it to come at all.

I knew all sorts of things that made time go by a little faster—reading a book, taking an afternoon nap, walking along the creek to go hunting up butterflies. But as for making things slow down, I couldn't think of much except counting stars. I figured that would take me forever. Papa always said there's more stars in the sky than letters in the Bible.

Sitting out on the roof of our porch, I started with the North Star, "God's Eye" as Mama called it. She said that's why it was so high and bright on the night the Virgin Mary gave birth to Jesus. God was real keen on seeing his baby boy and making sure people came from all around to do the same.

"Is that you, Nissa Bergen?" I heard a voice from down on the street. From the grackle screech of it, I knew it belonged to

Miss Chessie Roubidoux, the nosiest, meanest postmistress ever to read other people's mail.

"That's right, Miss Chessie, it's me sitting up here."

"Child, get inside the house before you fall and break your neck. ·

I had half a mind to jump down to the street and break hers, but I said, "I'm just fine, Miss Chessie."

"And what if you fall through? That roof is as old as Moses."

"It's good and sturdy, Miss Chessie," I shouted as I stood up. "See?"

Jumping up and down to prove my point, I set Chessie Roubidoux to screaming, "Heavens, child, you've gone as insane as your mother!" Running up to the porch I'd never seen her so much as step foot on, she yelled, "Ivar Bergen! Ivar Bergen!"

Papa was outside in a flash. "What is it?"

He must have heard me thumping up above because I heard him laugh, then say, "Nissa, that you on the roof again?"

"Yes, sir," I said as Chessie shouted, "Get your child down from there!"

"Miss Roubidoux, I don't see as how my child's actions are any of your concern."

"Well, if you want that child to go to ruin like her . . ."

"Stop there," Papa's voice filled with the heavy weight of anger. "I won't have you say a single word against Heirah. Not on my porch. And not in front of our daughter."

I smiled clear down to the pit of my belly as Miss Roubidoux turned her bony butt around and walked on down the road without so much as a grunt. "Thank you, Papa," I called down. He didn't answer, so I called again, "Papa?"

"Behind you, Neesay."

I turned. Papa stepped through the window out onto the roof

as I said, "You certainly fixed her wagon. I've never seen her just turn away like that."

"I don't think she's ever heard me raise my voice." Papa's face looked blue in the moonlight. "I scared her, I guess."

"She deserves a good scare. Something that shakes her soul up and makes all her meanness fall off like a scab."

Papa laughed. "If only it were that easy."

"Hmm." I nodded. "Thank you, Papa."

"For chasing off old Chessie?" He waved the idea away. "Don't mention it. I've been wanting to do that for ages, but your mama always beat me to it."

I walked over and gave Papa a good, soul-touching hug. "No, Papa, for being so good at your job."

Hugging right back, Papa said, "My pleasure."

"Is this a private dance?" Lara asked from the window.

"No," Papa stepped back, but kept his hand on my shoulder. "All Bergens are welcome."

It still seemed wrong somehow to be calling Lara a Bergen, but she was one all right and that ring on her finger proved it.

Lara stood next to Papa. He slipped his arm around her. When I wandered off to bed, Papa and Lara were still sitting on the edge of the roof pointing out constellations to each other.

Insanity

After school the next day, I walked over to the Carrolls' to see if Mary was ready to go pick flowers to sell at the dance that night. Mr. Cassell, who owned the Harper Hotel, had a dance every Friday night. He used to charge 75¢, but his price went down to 50¢ when they shut down the mine across the way in Mississippi. That closing cost a lot of people their jobs, including Mary's papa, but not too many mine folks went to the dance anyhow. I figured, and Mary agreed with me, that anyone who could afford 75¢ two months ago could buy flowers for his sweetheart at a penny a blossom. That kind of thinking had us outside the hotel every Friday night. Mr. Cassell wouldn't allow us inside if he didn't get a slice out of our profits, so we stood in the street, bowls of flowers at our feet, and pennies in our pockets to give out change. All our profits—which was sure to be at least a nickel because Winston Caveat, the fellow who married Mary's older sister April, bought his wife five ox eye daisies every Friday night—went straight to Mrs. Carroll who'd been reduced to giving only a nickel at church every Sunday now that her husband didn't have a job.

Mrs. Carroll was out front sewing up a pair of britches. "Morning, Nissa," she said as I stepped onto the porch.

"Mrs. Carroll." I nodded. I knew I didn't have to say another word. Mrs. Carroll had gone to talking to anybody who'd stand still and listen since her husband lost his job.

"Anthony's still living like we've got money coming in." She smoothed out the fabric she held to take a look at her handiwork. "He's running around ripping his clothes like we can buy new. Don't know what we'll do for school come next year. Mary's going to have to go through the dresses April left behind, I guess. And Teddy's even taller than Simon now. I don't know what I'll do for him."

Teddy was a tree with a sassy mouth—tall enough to touch the door jamb with the top of his hat. The only person taller than Teddy was Eliah Roubidoux, Miss Chessie's younger brother, and he's the tallest man I've ever seen.

"He says he won't go back if he can't wear decent clothes." She looked at me as if I knew where to find new britches long enough to fit a tree. "My son needs to graduate."

"Yes, ma'am." I nodded, feeling a little hollow. It didn't seem right to just stand there and listen, but there was nothing else I could do.

"I'll think of something." Mrs. Carroll bit through the thread. "I'll go see what's keeping Mary." Mrs. Carroll disappeared into the house, but I never heard her call for Mary. I suppose she lost that thought amongst all the worries floating around in her head.

A bit later, Mary came bounding out onto the porch in a dress with her hair dangling down her back. She even had her school shoes on. "Hey there, Nissa!"

"What are you wearing?" I walked around her to take a good look.

"Nothing fancy." She tried to act all modest, but she kept

smiling like she'd just won a cakewalk and claimed a triple-decker chocolate cake with coconut frosting for her prize.

"You can't go picking flowers in that." I pointed at her dress. "You'll get it all full of stickers and you could rip it."

"We might meet someone while we're out picking flowers," Mary announced. "I don't want to look like some crop-picking boy." She waved at my overalls, averting her eyes like my clothes were unfit to even look at.

"Who are we going to meet that's going to give an owl's hoot what we're wearing?"

Mary bowed her head, then did a weird kind of half turn like she'd gone soft in the hips or something. "Gary Journiette," she whispered.

"Gary Journiette?" I laughed. "The boy who wears britches so full of holes you could use them as a fishnet?"

"He does no such thing. Gary wears fine clothes."

"Are you blind as well as stupid?" I shook my head. "Just last week, I saw him walking down Quince Road wearing a shirt with the pockets flapping in the breeze like two string-tied butterflies."

"Stop trash talking Gary!"

"All right." I leaned in close so I could see the sweat on Mary's nose well enough to count each bead. "But in that thing your thighs will be sweating like a boiler tender in no time. I'm not listening to you complain about prickly heat for the next three weeks." As I gave Mary a piece of my mind, I noticed a smell. Not a stench really, but a nose-biting odor that struck me as a cross between pine sap and baking soda. "What is that smell?"

"Perfume."

"Per-what?" My ears felt like they'd been turned inside out. "Do you want every wing-flapping bug in Tucumsett Parish to be swarming around us while we're flower picking?"

"It's pretty."

"It stinks! And I'm not going anywhere with anybody wearing no perfume!"

"Fine then. I won't go picking with you, Nissa Bergen! I'll go all by myself."

"You do that." I turned and walked off.

I stomped down Quince Road with my bucket knocking me in the knees. God, what now? Do I have to give up my best friend, too? First Mama, now Mary Carroll. Everybody was leaving me in one way or another. At the open field on the far side of Sutton's Creek, I realized I'd cursed at God. Shaking my head, I tried to clear out all my anger. Just let it out into the air so it could fly off somewhere.

Dropping to the ground, I stared up into the sky. Why do people have to be so dumb? It was a question to God, really. My way of apologizing for accusing Him of taking my best friend away. He did no such thing. It was Mary who was leaving me of her own accord. Just like Mama. What I didn't understand was why Mary would be such a fool on account of Gary Journiette. No man's worth prickly heat and more bug bites than a toad's got warts. Why can't she just be the same old Mary and do her courting with Gary? Mary and Gary, I said their names in my head, then rolled over to bury my face in the grass. Their stupid names rhymed. Darn if they weren't doomed to be married off someday. I hated man-to-woman love— all that silly flirting, courting, and kissing. Not to mention the fighting, leaving, and divorcing part of it all. People called it romantic love like it was something spectacular, but for me romance was a kind of insanity you never recovered from. I prayed right then that I'd never look at a boy and think of courting for my entire life. Assured that I was safe from future insanity due to courting, I stood up, then set off to pick flowers all by myself.

Men Strain

In her last letter, Mama'd said she had a feeling God was fixing to send me a birthday present sometime soon. Said it'd be like most gifts from God, five parts puzzlement and five parts hidden blessing. Never did say what it was, just that I'd recognize it when it came along. Leave it to Mama to send me such a riddle then fall as silent as a church on a Monday afternoon. Of course, she did say she was brewing up a present of her own, but didn't so much as hint at what her gift was. I was left waiting and wondering.

God's gift came first. That's only fitting. But I wouldn't go around calling it a gift. In my way of thinking, it's an illness. It hit me like a bout of influenza that knocks you straight into bed and makes you wonder if you might be dying.

One day, I woke up real early, feeling achy all over and hot. Not feverish, just hot under the skin like I'd run home from Mary's. Getting up, I decided what I needed was a quick dip in the creek. Slipping into a jumper, I grabbed the towel from my washstand, then headed out the door.

In the cover of a purpley dawn, I stripped down to the suit

God gave me and slipped into the creek. The water cooled me a bit, but I was just as achy as ever as I stepped out of the water. Wiping myself down with the towel, I realized I was bleeding. I couldn't imagine cutting myself in such a private place. There was no sense to it at all. Grabbing my drawers, I realized they were spotted with blood as well. In a panic, I thought I must be bleeding somewhere up inside. I felt like screaming for help, but some part of me said to hold off. Maybe it was God telling me it was nothing to worry about.

Using the towel as if it were a diaper, I pulled my jumper on, then ran home like I had a demon on my tail. Before the front door slammed shut behind me, my mouth was open to call out for Mama. Little good that would've done me. Instead, I ran upstairs to find Papa. He sat in his favorite chair reading.

Out of breath and still wet, I shouted, "Papa, something's wrong!"

Dropping his book to the table, he got up to come to me. "What is it?"

Shaking, I told him, "I'm bleeding."

Closing his eyes, he took a deep breath and laughed.

"What's so funny?" I backed away from him. "I think I'm bleeding on the inside."

He took me in his arms and gave me a squeeze. "You are, honey, but it's normal."

"Normal!" I pulled back to look him in the face. "How can that be normal?"

"Your mama warned me about this and I just couldn't work myself up to talking to you. I'm so sorry, Nissa." Papa fumbled over his words like he was telling a joke he could only half remember. I could tell by the red in his cheeks that he was embarrassed.

"You knew this would happen and you didn't tell me?" It felt like he'd poured cold water into my veins. How could he not prepare me for this? And what was it? Did I have some sort of blood disease that was passed down in Mama's family?

Leading me into the bathroom, Papa said, "For some time now, I've been trying to find a way to explain all this to you."

Opening the wardrobe filled with linens, Papa put his hand on a stack of what looked to me to be diapers. Mama kept everything from when me and my brother Benjamin were babies, but I was surprised to see them there, just the same. With all of Lara's cleaning, I figured, the baby things would be the first to go. Papa patted them, saying, "See these here?"

"The diapers?"

"They're not diapers, Nissa." Papa took a deep breath. I could see that he was actually shaking. What could be so awful? He stared at the floor, then said, "They're for soaking up the blood. You pin them in your drawers."

Despite the nervous hitch in his voice, he made it all sound so natural, like a runny nose when you've got a cold.

That made me all the more worried. "Why am I bleeding, Papa?"

"Because you're becoming a woman and your body's making way for when you get married and have a baby."

I was only twelve years old. What did I need with baby-making skills?

Papa perched on the edge of the tub and took my hands in his. I don't know who was shaking worse, me or Papa. "When it comes to having children, Nissa, there are a lot of ways in which you have to be ready. There's the simple things like having enough money. Well, that's not so simple really, especially these days, but it's a lot easier than being ready in your mind. Knowing what to do with a baby and how to care for the little one—those things aren't easy in any way. But your body's got to be ready, too. And for some reason, the body happens to be ready first."

"What does baby making have to do with bleeding?" A storm started brewing inside my head. Like thunder in the distance, a memory came drifting in. I could see Mama crumpled up in Papa's arms in the garden, her skirt streaked with blood. I later found out that she'd started to bleed when the baby inside her died. "Did a baby die inside me, Papa? Is that why I'm bleeding?"

"No." Papa shook his head. "Heavens no, why would you think such a thing?"

"Mama bled when her baby died."

Papa pulled me close. I could hear his heart beating and when he spoke, his voice echoed in his chest. "No, honey, that's different. This blood . . ." He sat up, then said, "Oh, piss and vinegar." He stood and started to pace. "This is something your mother should be here for. She should be explaining these things to you."

Papa walked the length of the room, then spun around to walk back, looking like a tiger trapped inside a cage. I couldn't help thinking that Mama was the reason Papa paced the room. Mama wasn't there herself because she wasn't really ready to make babies. Her body brought me into the world, but two of Mama's babies died before they were even born and my brother Benjamin died when he was still a baby. Then there was me. Sure, I was born and more than half-grown up, but Mama left me because she didn't have what it takes to be my mother in a 'mama' kind of way. We were friends who did all sorts of things together—play-acting, chasing after butterflies, cutting out paper dolls, or reading storybooks—but she wasn't ready to be my mama in her mind. Instead of fixing on how best to raise me, she thought about ways to find her own happiness away from the ugly gossip-spewing folks of Harper. And in the end, she faced up to that fact by running off to live her own life up North.

Still, Mama once told me I was the best thing God ever gave her. She loved me. I knew that for certain, but sometimes I didn't feel it—kind of like the way Mama described a gift from God. My love for her was half puzzlement and half blessing and sometimes I didn't know which was which. At that moment, I realized just what Mama had meant by a birthday gift from God. Well, as far as I was concerned, God could have it back. I didn't want nothing to do with baby making, now or ever.

"Nissa." Papa stood still. "I've been reading up on all of this, but everyone's got their own ideas on what I should say to you. And I keep thinking about what your mama always said about lying."

"It makes your soul shrink," Papa and I said in unison, then laughed.

"Well, the truth is, that when a man and woman get together to make a baby, they exchange things."

Papa made it sound like they swapped simple, everyday things—a hairbrush for a rose or something like that—but I knew that wasn't what he meant exactly. "Like what?"

"Like . . ." Papa scratched his chin. From all the stubble there, I figured he'd decided to grow a beard to match his new mustache. "Well, you know how you've got to have eggs, and flour, and milk and all that to make cookies? Making babies is a little like that. The woman has the eggs and the man adds something called a sperm. Those two things together grow into a baby inside the mama. And you see, the woman makes eggs every month and when they're not used up in making babies they have to come out."

I felt like I'd been peeled from the inside—my own papa was telling me how babies were made and talking about sperm and bleeding eggs out of your body once a month. How awful! Whoever thought up this whole darn system was nuts. Why not just send babies to the earth in a cloud—Grandma Dee's version of the story was much better. If God could make Adam out of the dust and Eve out of his rib, he sure as heaven could come up with a better system than swapping insides.

"So I'm bleeding out babies?" I felt like crying.

"No," Papa shook his head. "It's like chicken eggs when there's no rooster around. The chickens still lay them, but they'll never hatch into chicks."

I had to laugh. "You mean I'm laying eggs?"

Papa tried not to, but he laughed too. "I guess you could say that."

"And it's going to happen every month?"

"I'm afraid so." He nodded toward the wardrobe. "You fold up one of those cloths, then pin it in your drawers. And when it gets soaked through, you'll have to wash it out."

"Like a diaper." And here I thought I'd done my duty with diapers years ago.

Papa nodded. He looked exhausted, his face pale, his eyes all red. "I should leave you to clean up then." Getting up, he said, "You have any questions?"

A whole swarm of them spun around in my head. Why didn't Mama ever tell me about all this? Do all women have it? Would Mary Carroll be getting it, too? Do you faint and pass out from losing all that blood? And just how do men and women swap insides? I felt like someone put my head on a lazy Susan and gave it a spin. "No, Papa."

"All right then." Papa kissed me on the forehead. His hairy chin felt like a toothbrush rubbing against my skin. "It's nothing to be worried about, Nissa. It's natural. Like men grow hair." He stood up scratching his chin. "You grow it, then you shave it off." He left the room smiling.

But I didn't think shaving was any one bit like bleeding out. Maybe you nicked yourself here or there and it was a real pain to have to scrape your face with a sharp blade every day—

another dumb idea. I mean, you take a butcher knife to someone's face and they'd call you crazy, yet men slice off their own
hair with a blade the size of a harmonica every day. But a girl's
bleeding time is a whole other thing. It's messy, smelly, and em-
barrassing. You never know if someone can tell you've got a
diaper wadded up in your drawers and you've got to find a bathroom every so often to change them. I hated it. The whole thing
was so dirty and filthy, I never wanted to talk about it again, but
Lara had other ideas.

After I bathed until my skin felt raw, I hid in my room. When I
heard a knock, I thought it was Papa, so I said, "Come in."
    Lara walked in the room and I felt like I'd been dropped into
a hot tub of water all over again. I pretended a dresser drawer
needed serious attention. Pulling it in and out as if it had a ten-
dency to stick, I made enough racket to scare a flock of crows out
of a field of ripe corn.
    Plopping down on the end of my bed, Lara said, "Feel like
talking for a spell?"
    "Not really," I said, surprised at how chirpy my voice
sounded.
    Out of the corner of my eye, I caught Lara looking around
like she might find something to say just floating around my
room. Finally, she said, "You know, growing up isn't anything to
be ashamed of."
    Letting the drawer hang out, I turned to say, "Awhile back, I
would've had no problem agreeing with you on that, but now,
I'm of a different mind on the subject."
    "How so?"
    "A few unsightly things have been thrown into the bargain."
    "What things?"
    Like she didn't know. "Well, insanity for one. I never figured

Mary Carroll would go crazy when she started thinking on boys as something more than . . ." Feeling all hot again, I shrugged, saying, "You know."

Lara opened her mouth kind of funnylike. The hitch in her voice made me realize she was trying not to laugh. "You mean, she's sweet on someone?"

"Sweet? More like silly. She's gone to wearing her Sunday dress to go flower picking. She even wore perfume. Next thing you know, she'll start wearing gloves!"

Lara raised her eyebrows. "So you've got objections to dressing like a woman?"

"All that stuff's just fine in church, but why's she got to go parading around the countryside in it?"

Lara shrugged her shoulders. "That's Mary's business, I suppose. What about you?"

"Any boy who has his eyes on courting me can take me like am."

"Sounds good to me." Lara smiled. "So you aren't bothered about becoming a woman?"

Lara might as well have been wearing tap shoes for all the dancing around she'd been doing, so I thought I'd just up and say what she meant. "You mean the bleeding?"

"That's right." She didn't so much as turn pink.

"I hate it."

"Me, too."

Can't say why, but I never thought about Lara bleeding out. Heavens, that meant she and Papa could have babies. The idea of it made me weak in the stomach.

"Do you have any questions? Anything your Papa didn't know about?"

I shook my head.

"You sure?" Lara stood up. "Well, I'll have you know, I'm here anytime you need to talk."

That is until she had babies of her own, I thought. Then there'd be no time for sitting around talking about courting and stuff. I couldn't quite decide if that'd be a good thing or not. "I'm just fine, Lara."

Lara came over and gave me a hug—felt a little like she'd mistaken me for a sack of grain, but I hugged her back to make her feel better. Tilting her head toward the drawer, she said, "A little wax on the bottom of that'll do wonders."

I forced a smile as Lara left. She tried her best, but all the talking in the world wouldn't make my new "gift" disappear.

After a week or so, I almost had the whole idea of it shoved into the back of my mind when Mary came racing over to our house. She didn't so much as say hello before she dragged me out into the garden. With all her pulling and panic, I knew it was something serious.

Plopping down on one of the benches under the cherry tree, she said, "I got the men strain."

"The what?"

Smiling just in the corner of her mouth, Mary said, "You know, the men strain. You go from being a girl to a young lady and you've got to start worrying about boys. Courting and cooking and all that. All that strain just makes you bleed." She laughed.

I didn't think it was funny, so I just frowned at her. "Well that's what my Aunt Claire used to say!" Shaking her head, Mary added, "I had no idea what she meant until now."

"You knew about this?"

"Sure," Mary shrugged like she'd known since she was born. "April's had it for years."

"And you never told me?"

Mary pulled at a tear in her sleeve. "My ma told me not to say anything. It's unclean for little girls to talk about it."

"I'll say it's unclean. I've taken so many baths this week I've become a walking pickle."

"You got it, too?" She grabbed my arm and squeezed.

Turning away, I nodded. In my mind, it was nothing to be proud of—gift or no gift.

"Know what this means?" She put her arm over my shoulder, then pulled me close, saying, "We're women now."

I looked at Mary. Her cheeks weren't as pear belly round as they used to be and she'd stopped wearing her hair drawn up in ribbons like a horse's tail, but she still looked like the girl I'd always known. "Just how do you figure that?"

"Nissa." She jumped to her feet. "Don't you see? It won't be long before we start courting. Ma says it's about time I learn to cook and sew and clean and talk properly to boys." Mary shrugged. "I'll just be glad to go to the dances on Friday nights like April does with her husband Winston." She twirled in circles like she'd just stepped into an invisible dance.

Watching Mary spinning with an imaginary version of Gary Journiette, I drifted back to the time Mama and I painted a wedding box for my Aunt Sarah. Mama took an old dresser, pulled it clean apart and put pieces of it back together to make a pretty, old box. After sanding it down, she painted it with trees and butterflies. My job was to plink little dots of color in the trees to give them blossoms. Mama sprawled out on her belly to paint, her fingers as steady as the hands on a clock, her eyes bright with some happy thought.

"What you thinking about?" I asked.

Tapping my nose with the brush, she said, "Seeing double."

As I wiped my nose, Mama added, "You can see the same thing every day of your life—a house down the road with a rooster weather vane that chatters a 'good morning' to you. Something you take for granted—like your toes. Then somebody comes along and steps on them. Like your Papa when he dances. He always steps on my toes and tells me when the weather vane's talking to me. That's what being married's all about. Sharing what you see."

Mama's idea of being a wife was sharing and that sounded fine with me, but I didn't see how it was any different than Mary and me looking at things. That is, until I realized how the baby making figured into all of that. Sharing a life with a man also meant bringing children into the world. I wanted none of that.

Standing up, I said to Mary, who was still dancing at her own private ball, "I'm never getting married."

"What?" Mary stopped.

"I'm not getting married." Picking a cherry leaf, I pulled it apart. "I'm going to be just like Miss Eloise Simpson, surrounded by friends and living out my life in a big old house on a hill where everyone's welcome."

Putting her hands on her hips, Mary frowned at me, saying, "Eloise Simpson made moonshine when liquor was outlawed. That's how she got all those friends."

I'd forgotten that part of Eloise's story. "So? Fact is, she's got more friends than a millionaire with a hole in his wallet and she doesn't have any family to mess things up."

"Mess things up?" Mary looked confused. "How do you figure families do that?"

"Leaving and fighting and dying and changing things all around—they mess up your life."

"And friends don't? Nissa, sometimes you're as crazy as your ma."

"How many times do I have to tell you to stop talking bad about my mama?"

"Oh, simmer down, Nissa." Mary shook her head. "You and I both know your ma isn't like other folks."

"And just what is wrong with that?"

"Nothing, if you're Heirah Rae Bergen." Mary laughed. "That's what I love about her."

"Isn't that just so." I smiled, thinking how Mama turned everything upside down and made it her own—a dresser becomes a trunk, an insult becomes a compliment, and a marriage becomes a friendship. I'd have to get her to teach me that trick sometime.

Mama's Gift

Walking home from school the next day, I noticed a crowd of people on the front porch of Minkie's Mercantile. They huddled together, pressing each other toward the doorway like the Minkies had decided to start selling wealth and happiness at six cents an ounce. The store was so full up with every child, woman, and man in Harper there wasn't any room to get inside.

Ira Simmons walked by the store with Otis Dupree. Ira just shook his head, but Otis got to laughing. Old Otis had a laugh, like the rattle of a train over the tracks, that made you stand and wonder where all that sound came from. Those two black men sure were getting a bit of entertainment out of all the silly white folks flocked around Minkie's.

I couldn't hear much above the din of whispering voices among the folks on the porch to catch the real reason why grown folks would act like crazy children after the last Christmas present under the tree.

Lara stood on our porch cupping her elbows and looking like

one of her precious gloves was on the mercantile porch being stomped to scraps. I waltzed over to her and asked, "What on earth's happening?"

"Your father's fighting with your mother."

Lightning struck me in the heart. "Mama's in the mercantile?"

I started to run, but Lara caught me by the shoulder, saying, "No, Nissa. He's on the phone with her. He got to shouting and people started listening in." Lara shook her head. "Vultures. I'd pay a pound of flesh for a private phone right now."

Pushing my way through, I heard folks just buzzing with all their gossip, but I didn't pay them no mind; I had my ears set on Papa. His voice was all muffled until I reached the inside of the store.

He leaned into the phone, shouting, "Heirah, you have every right to live any life you choose, but I won't have you doing anything more to ruin Nissa's!"

Ruin my life? Mama didn't ruin my life. I loved her. I felt like my heart was about to fall into little pieces. I could barely hear Mama's voice as she yelled back. Everyone was talking behind me. I ran to the phone booth, asking, "What's going on?"

Shocked, Papa leaned back as he saw me, then covering the phone, he said, "Nissa, your Mama and I need to talk."

"Everyone in Harper's listening. Why can't I?" I cursed Mrs. Minkie for ever taking the door off that darn phone booth. She said it got in the customers' way, but I knew she was just as nosy as the rest of Harper and wanted to listen in on folks' conversations. What I wanted was for the people in town to get out of my life. I wanted to squeeze into that booth with Papa, close the door, and find out just what the problem was.

"Not now, Nissa." Papa waved to get me to move away, but I didn't. I stood right in close so I could hear Mama. Her voice sounded distant, like a bird flying overhead calling out to all who'd hear.

"What is it, Papa?"

"Heirah," Papa sounded exhausted, like it took all he had just to say Mama's name. "Let me go now. Everyone's still standing around listening."

This time, I could hear Mama clear as a bucket hitting the bottom of an empty well. "Let them listen! I want my baby girl!"

The lightning was back. "I'm right here, Mama!" I screamed so loud my throat hurt.

Mama yelled, "Is that you, Nissa?"

Papa said, "Heirah, I'm going to let you talk to Nissa because I'm too mad to be sane. But don't you think for a minute that you've gotten your way on this account."

He took a deep breath, then handed me the phone.

"Yes, Mama," I said, grabbing the phone. Papa stepped out of the booth and I went in.

"Oh child, I've done it again. States away, I can still turn Harper onto its ear." Mama laughed and so did I. "Tell your Papa to chase those folks off with a stick. They're nothing better than a pack of wild dogs sniffing around a chicken coop."

"What's wrong, Mama?" I asked. "Why's Papa so mad at you?"

Before Mama could answer, I heard Papa yell something like, "Reise bort, dere skitten spioner!" I'd never heard Papa scream in Norwegian before. He kept right on yelling, but this time in English, "Go on home! This isn't a three-ring circus!"

"Is that Ivar?" Mama asked me. My eyes were fixed on Papa as he herded the townsfolk away from the store like they were sheep. Those folks looked as scared as Miss Roubidoux a few nights back. No one in town had ever seen Papa that angry. Truth be told, neither had I.

"Mama, what did you do?"

"I didn't do anything, Nissa. I just asked your Papa if I could give you your birthday present."

"What is it?" I was shaking so bad, my words came out all thin and quiet.

"A train ticket to Chicago."

"A ticket to Chicago?" I couldn't understand how a ticket to anyplace could make Papa so angry.

"That's right, so you can come live with me for a while."

Live with Mama. For two long years I'd been praying about being with Mama again. And here she was offering me the chance like it was nothing more than a piece of candy. "Live with you?"

"Indeed. We can celebrate your birthday together. You're getting to be a young lady now. That's a good time to be with your mama."

"But you didn't want to be with me, Mama." The words slipped right through my lips and felt like acid. They came straight out of all the pain Mama caused me when she walked out of the house one May without so much as leaving a note.

Silence answered me. I'd struck my mama dumb. I knew now why Papa was angry enough to take on the entire town.

"I'm not going, Mama. I won't leave Papa. It isn't right."

"I see that now," Mama whispered. She started to cry. "Forgive me, Nissa. I'm so sorry." As I heard her sob, I realized I was crying, too.

Just then, Papa yanked the phone out of my hand. He shouted at Mama, "What have you said to her? I won't have you doing this, Heirah. Think of someone other than yourself for once!" He slammed the phone down so hard, the catch cut his hand.

He was bleeding as he stepped back. Papa tried to hug me, but he was all stiff, his muscles tight, his skin hot to the touch. "Nissa, honey. I'm in no mind to be right to you." Papa stood before me, bleeding. His whole body shook. Tears streamed down his face.

The sight froze me. What could I do when Papa was at a loss? It felt like I had fallen into a pit and started plummeting through black air.

Doing What's Best

Standing in my bedroom windowsill, letting the wind that
rustled the garden below cool me off, I wanted to hear the reasons behind Mama's belief that I belonged up North with her. I
had ideas of my own floating in my mind. I feared if I didn't go,
Mama and I would lose what we had together. She'd drift off,
change into a complete stranger before I ever even saw her again.
She'd been gone just over two years. Her letters had stopped
coming and my mind had a hard time keeping a hold on certain things about her. Did she pick her teeth with her pinkie nail
after eating pork chops like Lara did? What was that sound she
made when she dropped a worm into a bird's nest? I heard it a
thousand times each spring, but I couldn't quite play it in my
ears anymore. Papa and I, we had a bond not even the end of the
world could destroy. But Mama and me, we were held together
by a string. I didn't want that string to break.

The idea of living with Mama pulled at my heart, but I
couldn't leave Papa. Every day of my life, Papa stood by—
helping me, loving me, telling me how much Mama loved me

when she wasn't there to say it herself. Still and all, I had to ask myself, even if it wasn't right, was going to see Mama the best thing I could do?

As the question teetered in my mind, someone knocked at my bedroom door. I turned as Papa took a step in. The stillness of his face told me he'd let his anger go. Clearing his throat, Papa said in a quiet voice, "I'm sorry, Nissa."

"You didn't do a thing, Papa," I said, sitting down.

Papa closed his eyes, then said, "A child should never see a parent's rage."

"It's all right, Papa."

"No it's not, Nissa." He held out his hand, saying, "Come here."

Putting my hand in his, I joined him on the bed under the starry night sky Mama painted on my ceiling for my twelfth birthday. Papa stared off for a minute like he had to chase his thoughts down before he could tell me what was on his mind, then he said, "Nissa, I always admired how your mama fought for what she wanted. Did what she thought was best, not what other people told her was the right thing to do. That takes courage. More than I've got sometimes. But Heirah took it too far today."

"Asking for me to come live with her?"

"No." Papa shook his head. "Telling me you should."

"Should I, Papa?" I squeezed his hand as I asked, half afraid he'd get angry all over again.

He squeezed back, saying, "What do you think?"

"Will I ever see her again if I don't?"

Papa jumped up. Walking to the window, he said, "Don't, Nissa. It isn't right to let fear take hold of you like that. You can't go running to her every time she calls for fear it's your last chance to be together."

There was an edge to Papa's voice, the way he used to sound when he came home yelling at himself for letting the car overheat for the umpteenth time in a row. It was experience I heard in his voice—the hard edge people get when they've been hurt once too often by the same mistake.

"Mama left you before?"

Papa bowed his head. "I wasn't going to tell you this, Nissa, but now I think it's best that I do."

Sitting on the windowsill, Papa told me, "For the first year we were married, your mama would walk out the door every other week." He shook his head. "First time it was because I pinched her in the backside. Said it made her feel like a roasting pig being tested for fatness. She came back after only a few hours, but the away times kept growing. Once, when I planned a trip to New Orleans without consulting your mama, she didn't come back for a week. After you were born, she stopped leaving. For years even. It wasn't until Benjamin died that she started up again."

I'd spent so much time thinking on Mama I could figure her motives faster than I tied my own shoes. "She couldn't face life as it was, so she left, hoping it would change."

Sighing, Papa said, "Now if only I would've figured that out sooner." He smiled. "Why weren't you so smart ten years ago?"

"I was three?" I smiled.

He laughed. "We've both grown up, Nissa. I've realized running after Heirah is like chasing the wind. You get all tired out and the wind just gets stronger."

"So I should stay?" More and more, I wanted to make Mama long for me. Make her wonder if she'd ever see me again. I figured it would serve her right.

"I don't quite know." Papa stared at some invisible place for a moment, then said, "A mother shouldn't be kept from seeing her daughter, but I don't want you to be hurt all over again."

"What happens if I stay here?"

"We go on living life."

"And Mama?"

He leaned forward and looked at me through his eyebrows. "I've given up on guessing your mama's behavior."

"You're getting pretty wild yourself."

Papa covered his face with both hands. His voice came through them all muffled, "Don't remind me."

Standing up, I decided, "If Mama wants to be with me, she can just come here."

Papa nodded. "Sounds about right to me."

Whether it was right or wrong or best, we waited to see if Mama would come to me.

Heirah Rae

Time trickled by. All weekend, I tried my darnedest not to even think of Mama. I set my mind on my birthday, planning out what I could do that day. Maybe Mary Carroll and I could borrow a fishing boat and take a trip down Sutton's Creek. We'd camp out under the stars and the whole bit. Papa always said we could go camping on our own when we got old enough.

At breakfast one Monday morning, my head was so deep into thinking on the fact that thirteen years old had to be old enough to be going camping alone, I almost didn't hear Lara when she said, "You know, my house isn't selling and it's a grand place."

I near about swallowed my fork when I realized what she'd said. "We aren't moving there. Are we, Papa?" I turned to him.

"Now wait a minute." Lara wiped the syrup spout with her finger, then sucked it. Pointing at me with the same finger, she said, "Don't go hating my ideas before you've even heard them. I deserve fair say."

What she deserved was to live by herself in that rambly house if she thought about moving there.

"Well, your mother is so proud of this house and her garden, it doesn't seem right for me to have them. Why don't we invite her down here to have the house back." Turning to Papa, she said, "And Ivar, you and I could move out to my house. Nissa could go back and forth from house to house whenever she pleased."

Wouldn't that be a state for things? Mama living in the town she put on an equal plane with hell just so Lara could live in her stupid house again. Not only was it the meanest idea I'd ever heard come out of a grown-up's head, it was the stupidest to boot.

And Papa thought so, too. He stared at Lara, his eyes squinted up like he feared they'd fall out for sheer surprise at her stupidity, then said, "I don't think Heirah would take to that idea."

"Take to it?" I laughed. "Mama'd rather see Harper burn, than to set foot in it again."

I said what I did mostly to spit fire at Lara, but I began to think it was the truth. When Mama came back to paint my night sky, she arrived after midnight. She didn't even come in the front door. I heard the skittering of rocks outside my window. Sitting up, I saw someone walking the ledge of the stone wall around our garden like a tightrope artist, hands out, skirts flowing, a suitcase of some kind slung over one shoulder. The moon perched on the peak of Mrs. Dayton's roof that night. It lit up the fabric of Mama's dress like hot wax in front of a candle flame.

I knew the night wall walker to be Mama right off. Who else would come into our yard in the middle of the night? Jumping out of bed, I ran to open the window, saying, "Mama, what on earth are you doing?"

Stepping in by going right over me, she said, "What's it look like? I've come to paint your ceiling."

"Now?"

Cupping my face in her hands, she said, "This instant!"

Mama said it didn't seem right to paint the night sky during the day. When the sun started spewing out ribbons of color over the horizon, Mama came down the ladder she brought up from the keeping room without so much as waking Papa. She said, "I'll be back tonight, Sweet Lark." Kissing me on the forehead, she went right out the window she came in and disappeared like a dream.

Papa didn't believe me when I told him she'd come until he saw the ceiling. Shaking his head and smiling, he said, "You ever wonder if your mama's got a little of the fairy in her?"

Giggling I said, "Maybe so."

Back then, that's the way I saw her coming and going at night—as magical. An added part of my present—like a bow. Now, looking back, I think all that coming and going under the cover of dark meant she didn't want any of the townsfolk seeing her, pointing fingers, and spreading rumors.

My thoughts started turning in on themselves, spinning over and over like a phonograph—Mama was afraid to come back. Afraid to live her life in Harper, Louisiana.

I didn't care if I never saw her again. She deserved to be alone. Who needed her. Not me, that was rock solid certain. Finishing my milk, I headed straight for school. No good-byes, no waiting on Mary Carroll. Making my way down Quince Road, I wished for a way to melt my heart down so it wouldn't hurt no more.

"Nissa!" I heard Mary shouting after me, but I didn't slow up. "Nissa Marie Bergen!" Mary came running up next to me, panting and sweating like a rock picker in the world's largest field. "Why won't you wait up?"

I didn't answer, so she said, "It isn't on account of that perfume, is it?"

My head was too full to even find words to say, so I just kept walking. Mary jumped in front of me. Putting her hands up in the air, she said, "Wait!"

Closing my eyes to keep from crying, I said, "Let me go by, Mary."

"This is about your ma calling, right?"

Turning, I thought to go into the woods and get away from her, but Mary would just follow me. "I suppose."

"What did she want?"

"Why? So you can tell Gary and he can tell all his friends?" Storming off to school suddenly seemed like a darn fool thing to do. I'd have to face the teasing the other kids had no doubt been practicing all weekend after they heard about the big to-do at the mercantile. No way was I going to be my mama's daughter. No one would call Nissa Bergen a coward. No sir, I was as strong and ready to fight as Papa had been on Friday night.

"I'm not going to tell anybody, Nissa." Mary put her hands on her hips. "Just who do you think I am? Last time I checked we were best friends. Or are you going to let a little perfume spoil all that?"

"We best get to school." I went around Mary to keep going. I had to face the other kids before I lost my nerve.

"Now, hold up." Mary grabbed my arm and spun me around. "I'll have you know, Gary goes fishing down in the pond be-hind Growers Meadow and if he saw me there in a nice dress, he might think about asking me to the dance. I heard tell he's been saving up money to do that same said thing. So, shoot me dead if I wanted to help him along."

"It's not that, Mary." I pulled away.

"Nissa," Mary was pleading now. I could hear the whine of it in her voice. "Tell me about it."

"She's a coward!" I stopped. Knowing I was close to shout-ing distance from school, I gave it all I got, yelling, "Heirah Rae Bergen is a coward!"

"Why do you say that?" Mary looked like I'd just said her papa had walked off never to be seen again.

"She left because she couldn't stand the people of Harper. They scared her away."

"Nissa," Mary took my elbow. "You aren't going to do anything stupid, are you?"

"Like what? Punch Peter Roubidoux in the mouth?" I shook a fist in the air. "I might as well do it before he so much as twitches a lip. You know he's going to have a lot to say once I get to school."

"I just don't want to see you hurt yourself."

Mama ran because it hurt so bad she couldn't stay. When you fall from a tree and break a foot, a doctor can make that pain go away. And when your body's got a fever, the doctor brings you round again. But where do you go if the hurt's inside your heart? The best thing you can do is leave what hurts you. Made sense to me. Harper filled Mama with sorrow, so she left it. And me in the bargain.

I couldn't go hating her without hating myself and where would that get us in the end? Alone and sad—that's where.

"Nissa?" Mary gave my elbow a tug. "You all right?"

Was I? All right enough, I guess. I couldn't just stand there for the rest of my life feeling sorry for myself, so I turned toward the schoolhouse and started walking. "I guess so."

With all our talking and carrying on, Mary and I made ourselves late for school. That suited me just fine because it meant all the other kids had already been called into the schoolhouse. There's be no school-yard standoff with Peter Roubidoux, Miss Chessie's nephew, who had a mouth twice as big and a heart half as small.

The room filled with snickers and whispers as Mary and I walked in. The schoolhouse could have been a chicken coop for all the noise those kids made. I didn't pay them any mind. Keeping my eyes on the desk I shared with Mary, I waltzed right by them, making them into bees in my mind's eye—nothing more than a buzzing swarm of insects. If I didn't go getting excited, they wouldn't sting me.

Mrs. Owens thwacked her desk with a ruler, "Quiet down. This isn't the front yard of a church, children."

As the class started to fall silent, Missy LaFavor leaned over the aisle to say to me, "I hear Mr. Hess over at the *Gazette's* going to start up a column this week, called 'Heirah's Follies.'"

Peter called back, "Each week, we'll hear all the loony-brained things Heirah Rae Bergen's done."

"Who needs the picture shows, when we got Heirah Rae and her crazy little daughter?" Teddy Carroll, Mary's blockhead brother, said from the back row.

"Buzz, buzz, buzz," I chanted to myself to keep their words out of my head.

"That's enough back there!" Mrs. Owens shouted. "I said pass your math homework forward."

Forward, backward, upside down, I felt like I was being pulled in every direction like a tarp stretched over a hole in the roof to keep out the rain during a storm—all that water weighing down on me until I felt the sag of it in my soul.

Was I a coward for keeping quiet? Or a better person? Papa always said it takes the patience of a saint to wait out a taunt and the fire of a demon to strike back. Well, I had the devil in me that morning because I had half a mind to rip the top off my desk and wallop Peter upside the head with it, then get Missy LaFavor on the way down. I knew well and good that Mary would see to it that Teddy got what was coming to him when he went home. Still, I kept my seat and wished I had a little more of Mama in me. She'd know what to say to those no-good lie-spewing cretins.

But the right words stayed out of my mind's reach. I crowded them out with numbers by working on my math assignment. Scrawling the numbers made me wish things were as clean in life as numbers tend to be. You add, you take away, you multiply and divide, but the numbers are always the same. They never change like people do.

Thinking how it might be nice to be a number seven, I heard the mourning-dove whine of the front door. People started whispering, "Who is it?"

I looked up. The sun full on the person's back, it looked like a shadow standing there, sunlight poking around the edges, trying to get by.

"Can I help you?" Mrs. Owens turned to the door, squinting her weak eyes.

"No ma'am." Those two words hit me in the heart. It was Mama.

Motherhood

Mama stepped into the room, her boots coming down with a stomp. Had she heard Papa and me talking about her the other night? Taken our decision as a challenge to come down to Louisiana and face the folks of Harper?

I didn't move as she came across the room in a pair of britches and a button-up blue shirt, looking like she'd gotten dressed out of Papa's closet. Everyone started chattering away, but I didn't hear a word. My eyes and ears were fixed on Mama.

"May I speak to you for a minute, Miss Bergen?" Mama stopped at my desk and held in a smile, her lips curling up at the edges.

Mama was a fool if she thought I didn't recognize her in that odd getup. Even with her long brown hair pulled up under a straw hat, she still looked like Mama. I only nodded. The words kept getting lost inside my head before they could travel down to my mouth.

"Then let's take a walk." Mama turned and started for the door before I could even move.

"Mrs. Bergen," Mrs. Owens stammered. "It's not customary to take a child out of school in the middle of the day."

Mama laughed, "Who gives a turkey's feather about customs, Mrs. Owens?" Holding the door open for me, Mama added, "And it's Heirah Russell now. Same as before."

Mama had changed her name back, turned "Mrs. Bergen" over to Lara Ross like it was a pie tin she'd borrowed. Mama and I didn't even have the same name anymore. I felt like she'd divorced me as well as Papa.

Stepping outside, I squinted into the sun. There was a stampede to the front door as the other kids got up to watch us leave. You'd think we were a freak show at the county fair, the way they were pressing up against the door. We walked away to the tune of Mrs. Owens's shouts to get the kids back into their seats.

Mama watched her feet as she walked. They looked large enough to knock out a gator in those big leather boots. "When I tried to figure out just how a young lady goes about courting, I did it all wrong. Larry Singleford asked me if he could sit on my porch for a spell and have some lemonade, I said, 'Sure thing, Larry,' then went fishing."

For a second, I almost laughed, then I remembered just what Mama had come for—to drag me away from Papa.

Kicking a rock, Mama stopped, saying, "I didn't much care how I was supposed to act. I just did what I wanted to do."

I didn't take to how Mama just walked on into school to get me after everything she'd done, then started talking about courting like she'd just been over at the mercantile buying half a pound of sugar. "You came all this way to tell me you were lousy at courting?"

"No." Mama frowned. "I came to say I've never been good at doing things the proper way."

"And that's supposed to be news to me?" I'd seen Mama read

49

the Sunday newspaper by spreading it out on the floor, then reading it one page at a time, regardless of the order; eat a tomato like it was an apple; pick cherries by spreading a sheet on the ground, then swinging from a branch to shake them loose—Mama didn't do anything the way it was meant to be done, except maybe breathe.

"You've sharpened your tongue since I left." Mama looked at me kind of sideways like she was deciding on something.

"What do you want me to say, Mama? Welcome home?"

"Hell no." Mama spit the words out. "This will never be my home again if I live to see the end of time." Taking me by the shoulders, she stopped. "Heavens, you've grown."

I realized I was tall enough to stare Mama in the chin. When she left, I was barely tall enough to touch the top of her head. I said, in a warning sort of way, "Mama."

"I'm here to say I've got a lot to learn about being a proper mama and I want the chance to try."

"You can't fry a chicken twice, Mama." I'd heard Grandma Dee use that phrase when she tried to show me how to sew and I cut the sleeve off a pattern or some fool thing.

Mama threw her head back and laughed like a dog howling at the moon. "Isn't that the truth. But who's the chicken in this case? Me or you?"

"I do feel burned, Mama. Inside." I tapped my chest.

"Motherhood isn't cooking, Nissa. You spend a lifetime getting it right." Mama looked off toward town. "Now that I finally feel like I'm living in my own home, it's empty."

"You didn't feel like you had a home here in Harper?" I thought back to how hard Lara had tried to make Mama's house her own and it made me feel small to think Mama never claimed it in the first place.

"People know less about what goes on in a grain elevator than they do about what happened inside my own house. Felt like I lived with the entire damn town inside my own walls."

It always did seem like the people of Harper could see through walls. Folks in town started talking about Mama's murals not more than half a day after she painted one. Now how did they know about them? Not one could be seen through a window that faced the street. And the wall around our garden was higher than the roof of our front porch. The townsfolk did have their secret ways into our house and that didn't just scare Mama. I often wondered if they'd learn to read minds one day.

"So you want me to come live with you?" I twisted the skin over my wrist, waiting for her answer.

Mama stared up at the sun, saying, "Your papa is a natural man. He takes to things as if he's done them his whole life. Never read a book on how to run a printing press, let alone fix them, but he keeps that newspaper office running year after year. Best damn husband a woman could ask for." Mama shook her head. "You and him could be together a million miles apart."

"What's that supposed to mean?"

She leaned forward so we were eye to eye. I could feel the heat of her on my skin like I was standing too close to the oven. "If you came home and there wasn't a trace left of your papa, what would you think?"

My answer came before any thoughts passed through my mind. "He'd been taken."

"And me? When you came home and found I'd gone, did you ever wonder if maybe someone had come in and carted me off?"

Not for an instant. I knew Mama had made the choice to walk out that door, something Papa would never do. If souls could take another form, Mama's would be the wind with a destructive force as strong as fire and the skill and beauty to make tall trees dance. Now Papa, he'd be more like a tree, rooted down so deep he'd be tapping on the devil's ceiling, but his branches would be far flung and full of chippering creatures of all kinds. I guess that'd make me a bird, flying from the tree into the wind. It sure did feel that way sometimes.

Mama nodded. I wore my answer on my face, I guess. "You know your papa is there for you. Not me. I'm not to be trusted. That's my fault, but it doesn't have to be true forever."

"So you're asking me for a second chance?"

"Second?" Mama laughed, then bit her lip. "You're a lousy count, Nissa, but I guess that'll do."

Stepping around Mama, I thought of leaving Harper. The only time I'd really left home was when Papa took Mama and me up north to Buffalo so he could pick up the printing press Mr. Hess had bought. I never much thought about other places. They were always outside and over there—a blank spot in my mind I never cared to fill. And the idea of spending time without Papa left me cold inside. But it seemed to me that Mama had the same notion I did about our relationship—which made losing what we had together all the scarier.

"Papa won't like it," I said without turning around.

Mama put her arm around me. It felt heavy on my shoulder. She said, "That's because I handled it all wrong. But together, we'll help him understand."

Walking down Quince Road, I realized just how unfamiliar Mama was to me. Not just her strange clothes or the way the boots made her walk all heavy, but even her smell seemed different. I remembered her smelling of sugary vinegar, but now the scents I caught hold of were those of paint, thinner, and a sliver of slightly rotten hay.

Her arm over my shoulder, Mama walked right past the post office, crossed the street without even the hint of a pause, then walked on into our house like she never left. Papa was still over at the newspaper office, so only Lara was home. Mama went straight to the kitchen where Lara stood finishing up the breakfast dishes. Leaning on the door jamb, Mama said, "I like your new dishes, Mrs. Bergen. I guess you could say they're elegant."

I didn't like the way Mama was smiling as if she'd just told a joke.

Lara near about dropped one of her new plates with the little yellow flowers along the rim. "Heirah!"

"Sorry to just waltz in here, but it didn't seem quite right to knock."

"Oh." Lara put the plate down and started wiping her hands on the towel like they'd been covered in mud or something. "Welcome. How long you staying?" I'd never seen Lara so nervous and I didn't like it one bit. She got all chattery and silly. "Shall I make up a room?"

"I could sleep in the garden for all it matters." Mama walked over to her mural. Running her hand over a patch of pansies that was fading in the sunlight, she said, "Won't be long before the paint starts to chip. You should paint over it."

"No," I said, stepping into the room.

"Nissa's right, Heirah." Lara sat down. "It makes the room so much bigger."

Mama stared off into the garden she'd painted. "Used to be a time I could stand here and smell the flowers. I never planted any of them in my garden. Why duplicate what you've already got?

"Should I go get Papa?" Something about waiting the whole afternoon with Lara and Mama made me feel itchy inside and out.

"Fine with me," said Mama.

"You think he'll be upset about you going into Mr. Hess's office like that?" Lara asked me.

Mama blew on her lips. "That old steam engine can spout and spew for all I care. Ivar's got a life of his own that doesn't know the boundaries of mine and yours."

"But I was talking about Ivar. Will it upset him?"

Mama raised her eyebrows, then smiled. "I guess we won't know till Nissa goes over there, will we?"

"I'll be right back." Walking out of the house, I couldn't help feeling like I should've stayed to protect Lara from Mama. I knew how scary she could be from time to time.

I took the stairs up to Papa's office at a run. Midstride, I realized I was taking the steps two at a time, just like Papa. That made me smile.

"Nissa!" Mr. Hess shouted from the other side of the room— half hidden by the massive printing press. "What brings you here in the middle of the morning?"

"Morning, Mr. Hess. I've got to talk to Papa."

"Of course, I hope there's nothing wrong." Mr. Hess followed me as I walked to the back office. He was as gossip hungry as the rest of Harper.

"Nothing, Mr. Hess," I said as I slipped into Papa's office, closing the door behind me.

Papa sat leaning over a table, lifting letters out of a box to set them into a sled for printing up an article. Those letters were as tiny as bugs and hard to keep a hold of, so I waited until he slipped one into place before talking. "Mama's here."

I could have poured cold water down his back for how stiff Papa went. "Here, now?"

"Yes, sir."

"Well, that didn't take her long." He turned to me, smiling. "What now, Nissa Marie?"

"It's my choice?"

Papa put his hands on his knees, saying, "You're too old for your Mama and me to be making decisions about you for ourselves. I want to know what you think."

Running my finger through the dust on his bookshelf, I said, "School's out in another week. My birthday's in two. I could spend some time in Chicago, I guess."

"Are you saying that because it's what your Mama wants? Or it's what you'd like to do?"

Staring at the floor, I whispered, "I wish I knew."

Papa stood up. "Trains run in both directions, Nissa. If it's the wrong choice, you can make a new one."

Room

Coming down the steps from Mr. Hess's office, I expected to see a crowd of people in the street, standing around and waiting to catch a glimpse of Mama. But only the Thibodeaux brothers hung about. Merle sat on the bench under the Minkies' window tugging at a hole in his boot like making it bigger would be an improvement. Clem leaned against the side of the mercantile examining the button on his left cuff. I spotted them for spies right off. They had no call to be sitting out on the mercantile porch when they had a sturdy porch of their own hanging off their feed store two doors down, but that would only give them a spy's eye view of the Carroll house, not ours.

Using the charms my mama taught me, I waved, then said real cheerylike, "Hello, Thibodeauxes! You come calling to say how do to Mama?"

I heard Papa swallow a laugh as Clem stared at me like I'd offered to skin his cat. "No, young lady, we're waiting on an order from the store."

"Of course you are." I nodded. Stepping onto our porch, I added, "Have a nice day now!"

Papa herded me into the house, then burst out laughing as soon as the front door closed behind him. We checked over our shoulders. Sure enough—fingered as spies, the Thibodeauxes headed back to their own porch, Clem's head shaking as he went. I could just about hear him complaining away. Merle walked along beside him, his mute lips as still as ever.

"Nissa," Papa shook his head, tears streaming down his face. "Promise me you'll save comments like those for special occasions."

"All right, Papa." Stirring up the bees of Harper meant somebody was bound to get stung, so you had to plan your attacks accordingly.

Lara came into the hallway looking like she'd been picking cotton all day, her face red and coated with sweat, her hands shaking. Even her smile wobbled. "Look who's here, Ivar."

Mama stepped out of the kitchen, a piece of pie in her hand and a ring of blueberry juice around her lips. "Your wife makes a tasty blueberry pie, Ivar."

Papa's face squeezed into a look of confusion. "Why are you wearing britches?"

Licking her lips, Mama said, "Keeps the men guessing."

Her answer did nothing to smooth out the wrinkles in Papa's expression.

Mama smiled, adding, "Besides, britches are easier to travel in. Your thighs don't stick together when you sweat and you don't have to keep your knees together for hours at a time. Truth be told, I should've started wearing britches way back."

As Mama walked toward us, I remembered how her skirts used to float up when she danced or took a quick turn around a corner. It didn't seem right for her to be wearing britches. More like she was hiding a part of herself.

Rubbing the back of his neck, Papa said, "So you came to get Nissa."

Mama set the pie down on the coat-whatever-it-was by the door, then slapped her hands clean, saying, "Not exactly. I came to set things right. If I can."

"How so?" Papa stood by the front door, the sunlight turning the hairs on the back of his neck blonde.

"By asking instead of telling."

I started to think Mama had her own spies in our house—coming down to Harper like she did and knowing how angry Papa was about her telling him what to do.

"I figure you don't owe me more than the room to breathe, Ivar. Not that it's my way of doing things, but as I see it, I should be asking what you'll agree to, not telling you what I want."

Mama and Papa stared at each other a moment, each one saying things I couldn't hear through their eyes. Everything went quiet, the air started to get heavy, then Lara piped in, saying, "Should we go out to the garden or into the parlor to discuss this?"

Mama kept her eyes on Papa as she said, "What on earth for?"

"To talk things out." Lara came up so she was standing alongside Papa and facing Mama. "As adults." She smiled at Mama, then nodded toward me.

Mama laughed. "Are you trying to protect my child's innocence, Lara?"

"She's still a child, Heirah."

"Lara." Mama took a step toward her. "I'm sure there's a thing or two I can learn from you. Cooking blueberry pie, for instance. But I won't take any advice on how to act in front of my daughter, thank you very much."

Lara's jaw tightened. She was holding words back. Papa took her hand. I felt like I'd been divided into pieces.

"I wasn't trying to tell you what to do, Heirah." Lara's voice seemed to fill up with metal as she spoke. Her words got all stiff and hard. "I was offering a suggestion."

Papa spoke before Mama could part her lips, saying, "Heirah, you and Nissa have had your time to reach an understanding, but you and I haven't. I'd like that chance, if you don't mind." Letting go of Lara's hand, Papa held his out to Mama. "How about a walk along Sutton's Creek?"

Still fool enough to wish Mama would take Papa's hand, my heart sank just a little when she walked right past him to the front door, saying, "That's a grand idea, Ivar."

Papa followed her out the door. They walked across the street side by side. From the back, they didn't look all that different from the Thibodeaux brothers on their way to the feed store. Papa called back, "We'll be back shortly."

Lara cupped her elbows, then said, "Your mama could burn the devil with that tongue of hers."

If I hadn't been deep in a wish that I could follow Mama and Papa to hear what they said, I would've had a thing or two to say to Lara. Instead, she walked back into the kitchen and I smooshed what was left of Mama's blueberry pie on my way upstairs.

Papa's "shortly" turned out to be of Biblical proportions—after all, a day isn't even the blink of an eye for God. The house was filled with evening shadows by the time I heard the screen door slam shut. The heavy stomp of Mama's boots told me they'd come back. I got up to run down and meet them, but I heard Mama coming up the stairs and decided I wanted her to find me.

She didn't knock, she just walked right in. Mama never did

take to closed doors. "Well, now I know what they mean by 'if at first you don't succeed buy a new brand.'"

Mama'd quoted the slogan for a detergent they made in Biloxi, but I didn't see how it applied. "What do you mean?"

"Lara Ross." Mama said it like I'd missed the obvious, and I guess I had. "Didn't she used to wear gloves and stockings to church?"

"Everywhere." I rolled my eyes.

"And this house looks like it's been turned into a hotel or something. Everything in its place. I swear she'd sprout horns if a picture on the wall went crooked."

Mama opened my windows wider to let the cool evening air come in. She stopped at one window to look out into the garden. In a gust of wind, the curtains floated up around her. For a second, I wished I had that picture painted on my wall. She looked as at home as she ever did to me.

"Do you think he's happy?" Mama whispered.

Walking up to the window, I saw sadness in Mama's eyes. Or was it jealousy? I couldn't tell right off.

"I suppose so." Papa was a bit like a tree in that regard as well. Over the years, he changed so slowly, you hardly noticed it at all. "He doesn't seem much different."

"Nothing much does around here." Mama slapped her thighs.

"You and Papa work things out?"

Mama nodded. "You'll be coming with me after your birthday party."

"You're staying here for two weeks?"

Mama gave me a nudge. "And just what's wrong with that?"

"You hate it here."

Mama stood up. "True enough. But that garden looks a fright. It'll take me about that long to straighten it."

"Want some help?"

"Wouldn't have it any other way." Mama opened the door and I followed her into the hall.

Being in the garden with Mama was almost better than sitting in her lap on a stormy night. The dirt beneath my nails, the smell of flowers hanging in the air, Mama throwing weeds in my face, telling stories about the blossoms she touched—it was like drifting back in time. I could've stayed there forever. We didn't even go in when it started to rain.

Mama sat down and leaned against the stone wall letting the water drizzle on her. "I love rain," Mama sighed. "It's like God giving you a bath."

Seeing Mama there in the rain, I wished I could just pull together all the moments like that one and throw out the rest; I sat there and enjoyed the rain.

Then Lara called us in to supper. Mama went right into the kitchen. Wringing her hair out in the sink, she sat down.

"Aren't you going to dry off first?" Lara asked, staring at Mama.

Mama poured herself some milk. "What for?"

"You're dripping all over the floor."

Mama splashed in the puddle forming at her feet. "One of the joys of having a tile floor is that you don't have to worry about the water. In fact, I used to open the windows when it was raining on a good windy day and use the rainwater to wash the floor."

"I remember that," I said as I sat down.

"As I recall," Papa came in with a newspaper under his arm, "that was the day the two of you went skating around the whole house with wet wash rags on your feet."

"And cleaned the bathroom by having a soap fight." Mama laughed.

"That's right." My mouth filled with the bitter taste of soap. I'd never had so much fun cleaning the house.

"Didn't you get it in your eyes?" Lara asked, sitting down.

"In our eyes, up our noses," Mama said it like a song. "It was the cleanest we've ever been. Inside and out!"

Taking a big bite out of her corn bread, Lara shook her head, saying, "I couldn't imagine it."

"It's not that different from a good food fight," I told Lara. We'd once had a watermelon battle in her backyard. And as I thought about it, that was the most fun I'd ever had with Lara. "And you can't tell me watermelon feels good when it hits you in the eye."

"No." Lara smiled. "I certainly can't."

So Mama and I dripped our way through supper and we all talked about the garden. Mama asked after the folks at the Crocked Gator and church. Papa told her how he was thinking about buying a new car. Mama said it was about time, before he had to put pedals in to power the engine. I almost thought we'd have a good time together while Mama was in Harper. Then Lara had to go and ask Mama, "Would you like me to fix up the guest room down here or one upstairs?"

"There's a guest room downstairs?"

I went stiff in my chair, knowing how Mama would take to having all her keeping things dragged off to the dump.

"Yes," Lara said proudly. "I fixed up that old storage room into a cozy bedroom for guests to sleep in. It should be nice and cool being just off the garden and all."

"Storage room." Mama tapped her fork on the table. "Where'd you put all the things in that room?"

"Well, Ivar sent you all the paints." She nodded to Papa who stared at his empty plate, knowing Lara was headed into a hurricane. "And the rest of the things were mostly junk. I took them off to dump."

Mama's chair hit the wall as she slid back to get up. Crossing the hall in a flash, she flung the door open. Lara had painted the room white, but it looked gray in the evening light. My favorite chair sat between the windows. Lara'd covered the small bed with one of Grandma Dee's quilts. In another house, I would've thought the room was nice, sweet even, but in our house the place looked like an eyesore, a blanket hung up to hide a hole in the wall where a beautiful built-in cabinet used to be.

Mama stood there. I expected her to turn around with enough fire and force to send Lara running, but she didn't. Pivoting on one foot, she said in a whisper, "You can't have what you didn't keep."

"What?" Lara asked.

"I'm going for a walk." Mama left through the garden door. I ran after her.

"Mama!"

She didn't so much as slow down. Going through the back gate, she started down the alley toward the tracks.

"I'm sorry I didn't keep your things, Mama." I felt so guilty. Here all this time, I'd been mad at Papa when it was me who didn't keep Lara from emptying out Mama's keeping room.

Stopping, Mama stomped her foot. "Darn it, girl, what are you doing trying to take care of me?"

"What?"

"Who went after me when I decided to go down to New Orleans and take up dance lessons?"

"I did." I'd found her at the bus stop, sitting on her packed trunk.

"That's not your job, Nissa. I'm your mother." She touched her chest. "I'm supposed to take care of you."

"I'm sorry, Mama."

"Don't be sorry, Nissa." She smiled. "Let me fight my own battles and heal my own wounds."

"By going away?"

Mama sighed. "I'm not leaving, Nissa. I'm taking a walk."

"Uh-huh."

"I'd give my heart's weight in gold to have your trust back." She rubbed my shoulder. "Now, go on inside. Help with the dishes. I'll be back before the moon shows up for the night."

"All right." I turned and listened to Mama's boots slogging through the mud, then went inside.

The kitchen stood empty, the dishes still on the table. Standing in the downstairs hallway, I listened to find Papa and Lara. Their voices drifted down from above, so I went upstairs. The study door was closed, but I could still hear them. Going into the spare bedroom in the front of the house, their voices came clear.

Lara said, "I think it's a fine idea, really."

"How so?" Papa asked. I imagined him sitting in the old green chair in the corner, leaning his head against the wall like he did when he was reading a book, his feet propped up on the arm.

"It'll give us some room." The way her voice kept drifting in and out, I figured Lara paced the floor. "A little time to get to know each other."

"You make it sound like you married a stranger."

"No," Lara laughed, but she sounded more nervous than amused. "We'd just be alone for the first time. I think that'd be nice."

It sure didn't feel nice to know Lara figured she'd be happier without me around.

"And what happens when Heirah decides she wants Nissa to stay with her for good?"

Papa's words nearly pulled me through the wall. Papa feared Mama wouldn't ever let me come home? And Mama might really want to raise me by herself? I wished I'd just split in half once and for all so I didn't always have two different feelings pulling me in opposite directions.

"Heirah will send Nissa home when she gets tired of playing mother."

Lara's comment burned my heart, but it set a fire in Papa. He jumped up, yelling, "Heirah doesn't treat motherhood like a game, Lara!"

"Do tell," Lara snapped. "She left you and Nissa, Ivar. Walked right out. Now if that isn't treating married life like a game, what is it?"

"Self-preservation." I listened so hard against that wall, my ear hurt as Papa said, "It's people with small minds like yours that drove Heirah away."

"I take it back, Ivar. The more I learn about you, the more I think you still love Heirah Rae." Lara slammed the door so hard, it made the walls shake.

I shook, too. Everything was falling apart. For the longest time I'd wished, dreamed, and prayed Mama would come back, find out Papa still loved her, and drive Lara away. But that dream had switched into a nightmare.

Where the Pieces Lay

Mama kept her word. The moon had just peeked over Mrs. Dayton's roof when she walked through the garden gate. Her clothes smelled of cigarette smoke and file gumbo. From the smile on her face, I could tell the trip to the Crocked Gator had made her feel a whole lot better.

"Waiting on me?" Mama asked as she sat beside me on the bench under the cherry tree.

"Not really." I told the truth. "I guess I'm waiting for a decision to work itself out."

"What decision?"

"I don't know. That's what I'm waiting for."

Mama laughed, one of those quiet laughs that could be mistaken for a sigh. "Well, let me know if you need any help." Mama pulled her knees up to her chest and sat with me in silence.

I almost felt like I did after I went swimming for the day and my body still had the idea I was floating. What could I do? Go off to Chicago with Mama when Papa might be losing his new wife?

Stay here with Papa when I knew Lara didn't want me around? I found myself wondering if there was a mental equivalent of the Dead Man's Float—a way to trick my mind into believing I'd died so I didn't have to think anymore.

"Where's your Papa?"

"In the study." He didn't so much as make a sound after Lara left. I even waited in my room with the door open, hoping Papa would come in to talk to me, but he never came out.

"And Lara?"

"Who knows."

"You get along with her all right?"

"On occasion."

Mama tapped her foot. "She'd make me want to leave my bed unmade, my books on the floor, and the food where I'd spilled it. Just to loosen her up a bit."

I chuckled to myself with the memory of the smooshed blueberry pie. "Yeah."

I thought of telling Mama about the fight, but that didn't settle right in my heart. It seemed so weird to know part of Papa's life was private—none of Mama's business, yet I knew all about it. Not that I should, but I did.

Mama and I listened to the cicadas for a bit. We used to call them God's own power line on account of the way they buzzed like a charge of electricity. Then Mama said, "Are my eyes working right? Did I see a FOR SALE sign on the Carrolls' truck?"

"That's right. Mr. Carroll lost his job. They closed down the mine."

"You don't say." Mama shook her head. "It's like the devil's caught hold of the country's purse strings. Nowadays no one even puts out a help wanted sign for fear they'll get a line of applicants that wraps around the block."

"Mary says you'd have to go to the moon to find a job these days."

Mama laughed. "Just about that far."

We sat there swinging our feet for a bit, then Mama said, "You know, I might be able to find Mr. Carroll some work up in Chicago."

"Really?"

"We need a handyman around the place to fix things up. And with the way things are up there right now, bringing someone with me could be a mighty fine idea."

"What do you mean?"

"Well, anytime you put an advertisement in the paper, you get over a hundred folks answering it. Every one of them needs a job more than the next one in line." Mama shook her head. "Desperation like that often leads to lying. Mr. Keller, my boss, went through three handymen before I met him on account of the fact that men said they could fix things up when they really didn't know the inside of a toilet from the guts of a cow."

I laughed as Mama went on, "I've seen Jacob take his entire truck apart and put it back together like it was nothing more complex than a child's top. There was no room for lying in that." Mama tossled my hair, saying, "Besides, I couldn't have your best friend moving away on you on account of losing her house to the bank."

"Sounds dandy fine to me."

Mama and I talked like she'd only been gone as long as it took her to take that walk—not over two years' time. But I kept right on talking for fear thinking too much would ruin things. "Mary's gone sweet on Gary Journiette."

"You make it sound like she's contracted a disease."

I sighed. "Close enough."

Mama leaned against me. "Oh, Nissa, if romance weren't dead, you'd kill it."

I laughed.

Lara never did come home that night. Papa was standing at the stove with a spatula in his hand when I came into the kitchen the next morning.

"Morning, Papa." I'd had one of those nights where it felt like someone snuck in and turned me inside out instead of letting me get any sleep.

"Morning." Papa flipped a muffin. His mama, Grandma Nissa, used to fry muffins in a pan and make them in the shape of little people. Mama liked the idea so much, she made them that way, too. But I'd never seen Papa cook them. Was he lonely for his mama?

"You all right, Papa?"

Patting a muffin man with his spatula, Papa said, "You take that walk with your Mama last night?"

"No." I knew just what Papa was really asking me, but I didn't have the strength to tell him straight out.

"You came back inside then?"

"Yes, sir."

Turning the stove off, he sat down. Looking me in the eye, he said, "How much did you hear?"

Papa had a way of holding me in place with his eyes—giving me the feeling that no matter what happened, he'd catch me, so I said, "All of it."

Closing his eyes, Papa said, "Lara was right about your innocence, Nissa. You've got precious little of it left."

Papa might as well have painted my insides with hot tar for how guilty he made me feel. "I'm sorry, Papa."

He shook his head. "I'm not talking about eavesdropping,

Nissa. Though, it makes you no better than the Thibodeaux brothers, I'd have to say. What I meant was that you know too much. About me, Lara, and your mama."

Papa stood up and went to the sink. Looking out into the garden he said, "I didn't know my mama was dying of influenza until the week before she died. She pickled fish not ten days before that. I figured all the work of storing up food for winter had made her bone weary. Never would have guessed she was doing it for the last time."

I knew Grandma Nissa had died when Papa was just five. They hadn't left Norway yet. She never did get to see the Statue of Liberty like Grandpa Knut always promised she would. Papa hardly ever talked about her. I'd always thought it was because he didn't remember much, being so young and all. But now I wondered if it was because he hurt so much when he did.

"In my day, parents didn't talk to their children. The children played outdoors or in their rooms. Folks went about their day and talked privately in their bedrooms at night. Heavens, I suppose they still do. Your mama's kind of bent my view on the way things work."

"Knowing the whole truth can hurt sometimes, but you feel empty if you don't know all the pieces to the puzzle."

"Really?" Papa smiled his so-you-figured-that-out-did-you smile, but he looked tired and sad.

"I'd still be mourning Mama's leaving and thinking she didn't love me anymore if I didn't know why she left."

"Suppose so." Papa sat down. "But this business between me and Lara is different. Private. Understand?"

I nodded.

"Good." He squeezed my hand, then got up to finish the muffins, saying, "Your Mama said to send you over to the Carrolls' after breakfast."

Mama had gone over to the Carrolls' before I did, so I thought maybe she was telling them about her idea to get Mr. Carroll a job in Chicago. No one sat out front, so I went inside and followed voices to the kitchen. Seeing Mama sitting at the table, a cup of coffee between her hands, was like finding a monkey in an oak tree. In the seven years we'd lived next to the Carrolls I'd never seen Mama so much as step onto their porch, let alone sit down in their kitchen.

Mr. and Mrs. Carroll sat there with Mama, listening to her like she was telling the deepest, scariest secret ever told. I stopped, thinking I should go back to the porch. After all, Papa'd already shown me the trouble eavesdropping can cause inside your heart. But I heard Mama clear as day as I walked back to the front door. She said, "If you're handy with fixing things, the job's for you, Jacob."

Mama had a job for Mr. Carroll already? My ears burned for more information.

"What would we do with the house?" Mrs. Carroll asked, her voice sounding a bit like Mary's when she'd gotten herself up too high in a tree and didn't know how to get down. "I can't leave April now."

"I don't see why Jacob couldn't go up there his ownself," Mama said. "The room they have for the handyman isn't big enough for a whole family anyhow."

"You say it pays twenty-eight a month?" Jacob asked.

"With room."

"Right." Jacob nodded.

Sounding a bit more like herself, Mrs. Carroll said, "That's more than enough for the house payments."

Mr. Carroll said, "Yes, but we can't even afford the train ticket north."

"Let me worry about that."

"What's going on?" Mary asked as she came in the front door.

I hushed her and hurried her out onto the porch. I didn't want our parents to know I'd been listening. Outside, I told her, "Mama got your papa a job."

"A job!" Mary looked like she could float. "Where?"

"Chicago, I think."

Mary came crashing back to the ground. "We're moving to Chicago?"

"No. Just your papa. He's going to be a handyman."

"A handyman? For who?"

I shrugged. "I didn't hear that part."

Mary started to pace. "Your mama makes me crazy!"

"What?" I couldn't understand why Mary would be talking bad about Mama. After all, Mama'd given the Carrolls a way to keep their house.

"Every time she does something it's half awful and the other half great." Mary plopped down on the railing. "Sure, she got Pa a job, but he's got to move away!"

"It can't be for good, Mary. He'll come back when they open the mine again."

"Yeah, well, don't you forget we used to say your Mama'd come home someday, too."

Mary was right. We had said that. Mama never did come home. Not in any kind of way that made me feel like I used to when I was a kid—like everything was right and would never change. But she came back in her own way. Mr. Carroll would, too. As Mama used to say, "When your life falls apart, you've got to deal with the pieces where they fall." Mary and the rest of the Carrolls would have to deal with their papa going away. My papa would have to find a way to show Lara that he loved her, if he did. And Mama and I would have to rebuild our relationship, one piece at a time.

To Hell with Harper

"You know what I think?" Mary shouted as she stomped off down Quince Road ahead of me.

"What's that?" I let the question spill right out even though I knew she'd tell me no matter what I said.

"Your Mama's halfdevil, I tell you! Dragging Pa up North without us. Was that her idea?"

"Would you really want to go with him?" I asked, jogging to catch up.

She stopped to shout at me, "Think on it, Nissa. I'd be with Pa! And you."

"I'd sure like that, but I'm not looking forward to going North."

"Why not?" Mary started walking again. "Haven't you been wishing for time with your ma for the past two years?"

"True enough, but just think how you'd feel, leaving your home and your papa, going somewhere you've never been."

"I know how it feels to have to say good-bye to my pa, thanks to you."

There was no talking to Mary that morning. She wasn't listening and I guess I didn't blame her. I knew how it felt to have a parent leave—like having a part of your heart taken out and carried away.

But being away from home on top of leaving Papa scared me so much I got the shakes when I thought about it. Sure I'd been to a big city before, but that was years ago and I only remembered the hotel room where we stayed and the snowman Papa made in the park outside our window. Mama said Chicago had everything—museums, theaters, universities, buses, and even trains that are elevated off the ground to let the cars pass underneath. They had more people living in that one city than they do in over half the state of Louisiana. With all those people, places, and speeding vehicles, I felt sure I'd get lost, run over, or kidnapped. But the closer we got to school, the more I started thinking about the fact that Peter Roubidoux and his friends had a whole new round of ammunition with Mama's reappearance. Thoughts of those hooligans made going to Chicago sound like a good idea.

Peter stood on the big rock at the edge of the school yard looking like a dog guarding a junkyard. He shouted, "Hey Nissa! Hear your mama's already chased Lara Ross off! What'd she do? Cast a voodoo spell?"

Peter's Aunt Chessie was always going on about how Mama practices voodoo. I swear that woman's thoughts run sideways. She thinks the strangest things. If a black person so much as sprinkles a shirt with baking soda to soak up sweat, Miss Chessie's convinced a voodoo spell is in the works. Heavens, she accused Mama of casting spells by drinking hibiscus tea. Now she had her no-account nephew doing the same thing.

Stopping a few feet from the rock, I said, "What's the matter, Peter? You afraid of coming down here to say that?"

Peter landed in front of me. "Not one bit, Nissa Bergen."

Time had stretched old Peter when I wasn't looking. He stood half a foot taller. I near about stared up his nose with him standing there in front of me. When I had punched him back when Mama first left town, I didn't take the time to think of things like height, I just let him have it. This time, I couldn't help thinking his fist was half the size of my face. Not to mention the fact that I'd promised Papa never to hit anybody again.

"So tell the truth. Your mama got a voodoo doll of Miss Ross?"

"Her name's Bergen. Mrs. Lara Bergen." I decided to stand my ground with words, but starting with defending Lara's married name was a darn fool place to begin.

And Peter knew it, coming back with, "From what I heard, that name won't be hers for long."

"You know Peter, maybe that nose of yours wouldn't be so darn big if you weren't forever sticking it where it doesn't belong."

"If you weren't a girl . . ."

I wasn't about to let him throw that tired old line out to me, so I stepped up closer, yelling, "Does that mean you'd hit a boy for defending his family? How gentlemanly of you, Peter."

I heard someone hooting behind me. Was that a cheer or a sneer?

"At least my family's only got one mama in it."

That line sent a rush of madness right through my body. I could feel a punch coming on me right down to the tips of my fingers. Peter deserved to be on the ground nursing a black eye, but I held myself as still as a tree, speaking slow and quiet. "I'd always heard tell that when you talk trash, you are trash. Never did believe it until I met you."

I walked off. Didn't so much as turn my head. I went right into school and took a seat. Felt like I was walking through hot air so thick you could hang a hat on it—no sound touched me until I sat square in my seat. Then I heard everybody shouting and laughing, but I didn't let the words seep into my head. I knew now that the best way to snap the fuses off of Peter Roubidoux's wisecracks was to walk away. You can't yell at somebody who isn't there.

"How'd you do that?" Mary asked as she sat down.

"What?"

"Walk away like that with Peter shouting after you. Did you hear what he called your ma?"

"Doesn't matter." Peter Roubidoux would never change. Neither would his aunt or any of the other people in Harper who couldn't open their eyes to see my family for who we were. That's why mama left. She wasn't a coward. Nor was she a fool. Mama'd left because it was the only way to get those people out of her life for good. Suddenly, Harper didn't seem like home anymore. It was a stuffy, ugly place I couldn't wait to leave.

Finding Love

Walking home that afternoon, I saw Papa heading out of town on foot. Figuring he'd set a course for finding Lara, I went inside. The front door hung open as did the back. No doubt Mama'd left them that way when she walked out to the garden. Sure enough, she sat in the center of the stone path leading straight down the middle. Seeing me, she slapped a flag stone beside her, saying, "Take a seat."

I sat down facing the house like her. Mama stared inside as if she expected to see someone else coming along behind me. She didn't speak, so I said, "What are we doing?"

"I was weeding and I don't know why, but I looked into the house. A bird flew right on through the hallway, then out here to take a roost on the wall. Never seen anything like it." Mama pointed to the fence. There sat a sparrow singing away like she was proud of her new achievement.

"So what makes you think it'll happen again?"

"It's spring." Mama leaned into me. "And that bird isn't singing a lullaby."

Mama had a way of seeing things that made the impossible look probable, but I didn't believe we'd see any suitors for our little "house" sparrow. Still, I didn't mind spending a little time with Mama. Unfortunately, she shushed me anytime I tried to talk. My legs started to fall asleep as I sat there thinking how nuts it was to sit in your garden waiting for a bird to fly through your house.

Then it happened. A bird swooped down out of the bright sunlight beyond our front door into the shadowy tunnel of our hallway, its wings carrying it right out into the garden as it sang out to the would-be sweetheart on our back wall. There was no denying it. Mama did make the impossible happen.

"I don't believe it!" I said.

Mama started spreading the uprooted weeds as mulch, acting like she'd just finished washing dishes. "What's to believe? You saw it."

"Yeah, I guess." I got up to help Mama, my legs stiff and tingly. I didn't understand how Mama could just go right on with her day like nothing had happened. I guess she regarded the impossible as kind of ordinary.

After a bit, I remembered seeing Papa, so I asked, "Where was Papa going?"

"Off to talk to Lara, I suppose."

"You think she's out at her old house?"

"Probably so," Mama's voice had gone thin. It didn't have the bounce of music I loved so much.

"What's wrong?"

Mama held her hands up in the air, then let the weeds she held drop down. Some of them fell into her hair and onto her shoulders, but she didn't wipe them away. Turning to me she said, "I just want your papa to be happy, that's all."

"With Lara?"

"He could've married Eloise Simpson for all I care, just as long as he had a good life."

My mind said, "He could've had one with you." But I didn't let that out.

"You think Lara will come back?" I asked, amazed that I'd talk about such things with Mama.

"Who's to tell, Nissa?" Mama wiped herself off, adding, "You've just got to pray and let God handle the rest."

Staring at the open doorway and dreaming about that bird flying through, I couldn't help thinking love shows you the way. If you're not with the one you love, God'll lead you to that person if you just stop, listen, pray, and wait. That is if you're meant to be together—like Mama and me. I never did think it was right for us to be apart. But I didn't know about Papa and Lara. Seeing them together always made me miss Mama. Then again, Mama spoke the truth. Papa deserved to be happy. And who knew better than God what would make Papa happy? Nobody, that's who. So, I just stood there and prayed the right thing would happen. No, the best thing.

The trouble was, Lara didn't know Papa loved her the way he used to love Mama. In my way of thinking, love lets you see things in a new light and it's jealousy that blinds you. Lara couldn't see how low down Papa looked coming home that evening. Seeing a way I could help, I jumped right up and ran clear out to Lara's place. Stopping to catch my breath, I had to laugh at the thought of me going after Lara to get her to come back to Papa. I'd spent close to a year of my life trying to find a way to keep the two of them apart. Sometimes, I think God just sets things in motion, then sits back and laughs because He knows every crazy thing you do's bound to come back and bite you square on the backside.

I might've even been laughing when I rapped on the front door, but seeing Lara knocked any happy thought clean out of me. That woman could have turned St. Peter to stone with the look she gave me. If I hadn't been too scared to move, I probably would've turned and run all the way back home.

Lara didn't open the screen door, she just glared at me, asking, "You here to count your coup, Nissa?"

"Count what?"

"Claim victory."

I shook my head. "No. I came to say Papa loves you." I just blurted the words out like I was reciting the alphabet. In a less stressful situation, I would've found a better way to say it.

"And just who appointed you to deliver that message?"

"Me."

"I see." Lara folded her arms in front of her, saying, "Well, you've delivered your message, now what?"

She had me there. I had no earthly clue what to do next, so I kept quiet.

"There you go again, Nissa. Going in over your head, then waiting for someone else to come rescue you. One of these times there'll be no one there to help."

I felt pretty helpless right then, that's for sure.

"All right then, since you've jumped into this with both feet, I'll take you at your word. So tell me, what makes you think your father wouldn't just pack his bags and follow your mother to Chicago if he could."

"Mama would tell him not to come."

I told a truth I'd known in some part of me since the day Mama'd left, but it still hurt to put it out there in the open. Lara didn't even blink an eye, she just said, "But he would still want to go."

"I don't think so." I stared at the floor, wishing I wasn't standing there on that front porch saying the things that came flowing out of my mouth like they'd been lying in wait. "If Papa wanted to be with Mama, he would've followed her when she left."

I remembered Papa driving out to find Mama, but he didn't stay away long. Back then, he knew he wouldn't find her. And now I knew he wasn't really looking for her.

"But he came out here to find me. That's what tells you he loves me?" I heard an odd little hitch in Lara's voice. I hadn't noticed it through the gray sheen of the screen, but Lara had been crying.

"It's not just that. I can see how sad he is without you."

"Maybe so." Lara bowed her head for a moment, then looked up to say, "Thank you for coming out, Nissa. I'll say good day to you now."

She closed the door and disappeared into her house without saying another word. Standing there, my shadow creeping over the edge of the porch like it was trying to hide, I wondered if I'd done the right thing.

In the end, that didn't matter. I'd done it. There was no taking it back, so I walked back to town, dragging my feet in the dusty road, my mind drifting, and hoping Lara would return to her new home.

The Dance

That Friday, Mary and I picked a few extra baskets full of flowers.
School had let out for the summer and that first Friday was the only
night Mr. Cassell let the children into the hotel for a nickel apiece,
so a lot of the young folks came to the dance to celebrate. Peter
Roubidoux brought Missy LaFavor. The two of them deserved each
other. Peter came sauntering up like he owned the parish, saying to
Missy, "You're too pretty for one of those dried-up flowers."

Missy smiled real big and nasty at me. I wished I had a little
sting weed to rub in her eye. Then Peter tried to misstep right
into the basket by my feet, but I tangled my foot up with his. We
started kicking and dancing like two kids after the same can in
a hot round of kick the can. Finally, I got smart and stomped on
his foot. He started hopping and howling. Mary let out a laugh so
loud everybody looked our way. I could see by the fire in Peter's
eyes that he wanted to pound me good. But he took Missy's arm,
saying, "Let's get inside, it's starting to smell bad out here."

Mary gasped for breath, saying, "You whop that boy many
more times and he's liable to kill you in your sleep."

"How much for a flower?" I turned, and there stood Mama in a dress fit for dancing, all flowy and light—a pale peach that made me think of the orange-peel frosting Grandma Dee used to put on her carrot muffins.

"Here's one for you, Miss Heirah." Mary held out a yellow gaillardia as bright as Mama's dress was pale.

"Thank you, Mary." Mama took the flower, then went inside smelling it like she didn't have a thing to worry about. Now the last time Mama went to a dance at the hotel, Mr. Cassell had to re place a window. Mama didn't break it, mind you. She just danced a jig that struck Merle Thibodeaux as so funny, he laughed himself right out the window, in a manner of speaking. Merle's mute on account of the fact his voice box got crushed by a baseball when he was a boy, so when he started laughing, he looked like he was gasping for air. No sound came out. His mouth just went wide open, his eyes started to water, and he kept slapping his knees. His brother Clem wasn't around to clarify things, so Chessie Roubidoux went to pounding old Merle on the back. He stag gered away from her and fell back first out the window.

Folks didn't stop talking about that night for months afterward. And Merle, he started laughing every time he saw Mama walk by. Mama laughed right back. But all that didn't stop Mama from walking straight into the hotel. And here I thought Mama was a coward.

I sold flower after flower without even thinking of Papa until I saw Lara. Her eyes caught my attention first. Standing in line, waiting to get in, she was hidden behind a bunch of folks. I could only see part of her. Her eyes pulled me right in—as blue as the flower she had pinned to her shoulder.

Leaning this way and that, I could tell that Papa stood with her. The smile on Lara's face told me things had taken a turn for the better. Papa had won her over again.

As they came past Mary and me, Papa winked. I kept my lips shut and in a wide smile. Lara had her eyes on Papa with a look that said she was real glad to be there. And that made me happy, too.

Along about that time, April came up with Winston. He looked like his cheeks were about to burst from smiling too hard. "I'll take six daisies this evening, Nissa." He held out the money to me, but my eyes were fixed on April who on most days looks like a porch post that's sprouted legs, but that night, she'd sprouted a tummy big enough to hold a wee baby. Suddenly, I knew why Mrs. Carroll couldn't leave town and Winston had started buying an extra daisy.

Leaning into Mary, I shouted, "Why didn't you tell me?"

"Tell you what?" Mary asked, taking Winston's money.

"That Winston's got cause to buy flowers for two!" I yelled, handing Winston the flowers.

"What?" Mary stared at her sister in much the same way she used to when April got caught kissing a boy in the abandoned church on Charleston Road. Sounding as if she might choke, she asked, "You're having a baby?"

April leaned toward her sister, saying, "No, I've swallowed a beehive."

"Does Ma know?"

People made their way around April and Winston, as April said, "Of course she knows. She isn't half blind like you are!"

Mary stood there in a daze as April and Winston walked off. "A baby." She whispered. "I'm going to be an aunt."

"Congratulations." I slid my basket over to Mary, then said, "You sell the rest of these, I'm going inside."

Too stunned to protest, Mary didn't keep me from going inside, dropping my nickel into Mr. Cassell's till, and leaving her alone to sell the rest of the flowers. The hotel was filled to bursting that night. I had to weave like a fish through the rocks to get in to the dance floor. As usual the crowd around it was thicker than the crowd on it. Most folks in Harper preferred watching to dancing. That is, until people started loosening up under the weight of a few drinks. And now that alcohol was legal again, they weren't passing it around in Mason jars. Mr. Cassell even had folks who walked through the crowd selling drinks.

The dance floor had just opened, but the drinks already flowed—out of the kitchen, down people's throats, and, in some cases, onto the floor—all signs of a wild night in the making.

As always, Mama danced in the center of the room, her body flowing to the music. Grandma Dee says music beats in Mama's heart and I believe it. When the music starts, Mama's whole self goes into the dance, every part of her that bends keeping time with the band. Mama doesn't even need a partner. She can dance the night away without so much as opening her eyes. Many times, Papa would have to take a seat to catch his breath, but Mama seemed to breathe with the beat.

Folks would point and shake their heads, saying it isn't natural to dance that way. Anybody who ever spent an evening in the Crocked Gator knew that to be a lie. Mama often joined the crowd that formed when Mr. Otis Dupree blew a train whistle note on his harmonica. Folks pushed the tables aside as the band started shaking the walls of the Gator with their tunes, then the whole place exploded with dancing. Folks hollered and laughed, but nobody pointed fingers or cast verbal stones. If anything, they'd cheer each other on. Heck, I'm not even afraid to dance with the Gator crew and I trip over my own feet.

That night, Mama danced alone. Papa and Lara stood in a far corner, people pushing and walking right by them as they talked. Standing next to a table of food, Lara kept sneaking peanuts out of the bowl behind Papa like she hadn't eaten in a week. Mama'd made Lara so nervous she'd taken to eating like a horse with a tapeworm just to keep herself busy. Then again, she and Papa looked mighty happy. They didn't even come out of their corner but for a dance or two before they left not more than an hour after they arrived. Part of me wanted to follow them out into the street where I knew the night air was dark and cool, but my spying days were over.

A few minutes later, Mama came and grabbed me by the hands, shouting, "Nissa girl, you're behind on your dancing lessons. Let us make our mark on this here floor."

Sweating hot from just standing on the edge of the dance floor, my body felt like I'd collapse if I moved too fast, but Mama pulled me into a dance. I tried to listen to the music and let it work its way inside me, but my eyes drifted down to watch my feet stumble and my mind kept thinking of all the mistakes I made.

Mama shook me by the shoulders, saying, "Let go, Nissa."

I smiled back at her, but had no idea what she meant.

"Think of nothing!" she yelled.

The band played so loud I could feel the beat in my hair. If I'd so much as lift an elbow I'd hit three people, the dance floor had crowded up so. Plus, I knew everyone had their eyes on me what with Mama only a few feet away.

"Picture that bird flying through, Nissa." Mama's voice floated to me.

Closing my eyes, I let people jostle me as I pulled the bird's flight into view. For one hanging second, all the sound disappeared. Then the music started playing inside my head. Trickling down into my limbs, the beat moved me. Can't say how exactly, but my thoughts had notes. I don't know an upbeat from a downbeat, but I flowed with the music. Truth be told, I probably looked like a monkey fighting its way out of a sausage casing, but it didn't matter. I was really dancing.

"Look at my girl go!" Mama's voice hitched onto the beat and I danced all the harder, feeling for the shortest time like Mama's little girl again. And knowing, in a part of me that I didn't recognize yet, that I never could go back to being that girl dancing on her Mama's toes. That night, I wasn't just Mama's girl. I danced on my own legs and it felt good.

Family

Mary Carroll and I had a deal with Mr. Beaurigard next door. He left a ladder against his side of our garden wall, Mary used it to get up to my room, and we kept him stocked in fishing slugs all summer. Things worked well this way. Mary didn't have to go in through the front door and Mr. Beaurigard could limit his digging to finding the coffee cans he buried in his backyard to hide his valuables.

The morning after the dance, Mary came crawling into my window before breakfast. "Nissa, we made a dollar ten last night!"

"What?"

"You heard me!" Mary pulled her hands out of her pockets and showered my bed with coins.

"A whole dollar and ten cents?"

"I stood out there selling until well after dark. We sold clean out." Mary plopped down on the bed. "Which reminds me, I saw your Pa and Lara walking home last night, hand in hand."

Smiling, I said, "I know."

Mary leaned against the wall next to me, saying, "What you don't know is that they kissed."

"What?" I sat up.

"I was headed over to the mercantile to treat myself to a piece of saltwater taffy. As I walked by your place, I saw them in the front hall, kissing."

"Kissing?" I'd seen people kiss before. There's a peck on the check, then there's the kind that turns a person's lips blue. "Or *kissing*?"

"Let me put it this way." Mary paused, then laughed before saying, "Won't be long before Lara starts looking like April."

"People don't get pregnant from kissing."

"True enough, but when you start by kissing like that, baby making isn't far off."

"Ah!" I buried myself under my pillows. The thought of my Papa baby making made me feel dirty.

"They're married." Mary gave me a shove. "What are you so worried about? That's what married folk do."

"I know," I said through my pillow. Peeking out, I added. "That doesn't mean I have to like it."

Mary rolled her eyes.

I remembered baby Benjamin. I used to love the way he wrapped his fat little fingers around mine and stuck his tongue out when he laughed. I used to make him a hammock between two chairs weighted down by books. He'd swing and laugh until he fell asleep. Being a sister again wouldn't be all that bad.

"What are we going to do with all this money?" Mary asked, running her hands through the coins.

"Why are we spending it? Doesn't your mama want it?"

"Pa's got a job now."

"When we get to Chicago, but we aren't leaving until after my birthday."

"Speaking of which." Mary started picking up the coins she'd scattered all over my bed. "We could buy you a present." She shook a handful in my face.

"Give it to your Mama." I pushed her hand away. "Wait!" I grabbed her hand. "We can use it for your pa's ticket to Chicago!"

"Really?"

"Won't pay for all of it, but some." I started snatching up coins. Mary joined me, then we ran into the hall to bring them to Mama. She'd taken to sleeping on the couch in her old room. Spilling the coins onto the sewing table by her head, I said to Mama, "Here's our share of Mr. Carroll's ticket to Chicago."

Stretching, Mama said, "We're driving to Chicago. The Carrolls' can't afford the ticket, so I sold our tickets for gas money."

"Oh."

Mary pointed at the pile of coins. "That'll help, though, won't it?"

"Enough for a tank of gas at least." Mama smiled. "Now, get out of here so I can get the sleep out of my head."

"Yes, Mama." I kissed her on the forehead, then ran out with Mary close behind me. Most folks thought Mama had a pretty nasty selfish streak and truth be told, sometimes so did I, but now I remembered how generous she could be.

Mary went out through the back door to go home. As she headed for the gate, I heard Lara say, "How does she get inside?"

"Mary climbs the ladder in Mr. Beaurigard's yard, then comes in through the window."

"Sounds like something Tom Sawyer would do," Lara said as she added more water to the vase of flowers in the kitchen window.

I'd take such a comment as a compliment from most folks, but the way Lara said it made it sound like a bad thing. "I like Tom Sawyer."

"As do I, but he's a boy."

I rolled my eyes. Lara started laughing. I didn't quite know why, then I realized Papa was standing right behind me. When Lara said, "You two," I knew for certain that Papa had rolled his eyes, too.

"Muffin maker." I teased Papa.

"Window user."

We laughed, then headed for the kitchen. "Who's cooking?" I shouted, seeing Mama coming down the stairs.

"You are!" came shouts from all over. The whole house had the same idea, except for me. I didn't mind cooking, I was just so darn happy to have my family together. My whole family.

Roots and Walls

After school let out, I couldn't wait to get to Chicago. Sure my birthday was coming up, but I had one of those every year, no reason to make a fuss over just one. So, I didn't see a real reason to stay a whole extra week. According to Mary, Lara and Papa were on more than just friendly terms again. And almost as if Papa wanted to make darn sure he wasn't still sweet on Mama, they had a fireworks display of a fight on Sunday morning. The fight broke out after Papa asked when Mama planned on bringing me home. I saw the whole thing from my reading spot on the seventh step.

Mama said, "When she has a mind to leave, I guess."

"A mind to? What if that's two years from now?" Papa put the book he'd been reading down on the table next to the couch.

"Then it is," Mama said, walking out of the room.

Papa jumped to his feet. Following Mama out to the garden, he said, "I don't like the sounds of this, Heirah. Nissa needs some stability in her life."

"She's got you." Mama smiled back at him, but Papa wasn't pleased.

"You know exactly what I mean."

"Ivar," Mama turned to face him. "Nissa could hate Chicago and want to come home next week."

"Or?"

"She might enjoy herself and want to stay on awhile."

"What about school, Heirah?"

"Let's worry about that when fall rolls around." Mama spun her hand in the air. "Heavens, summer hasn't even worked up a good sweat yet."

Papa stepped real close to Mama and whispered in her ear. Mama's face shifted. Even from the staircase inside, I could see the rage building up in her eyes. Papa started to walk back into the house. Mama yelled in a voice that could tear through a person's insides. "Don't you ever threaten me, Ivar Knut Bergen!"

"I didn't threaten you, Heirah." Now it was Papa's turn to be calm and quiet. Somehow when Papa yelled it didn't scare me unless he'd gone out of control like he did over at the mercantile, but that was a once-in-a-lifetime thing. Now when Mama got mad, I half believed the earth would shake.

Mama was up the back steps and in Papa's face in a flash. "You will never take my little girl away from me."

"You did that on your own."

Mama hauled back and hit Papa square in the jaw. She didn't slap him. She slugged him. Papa's head snapped back. I screamed out for him.

Lara hurried into the hallway, but she didn't go toward Papa. Everyone stood still waiting for Papa to react. He licked his lips, the bit of blood there disappeared under his tongue. "Proud of yourself now, Heirah?"

"God forgive me," Mama whispered. She turned, then wandered out the front door.

I'd never known Mama to strike another living thing. I ached with the thought of her hurting Papa, but I couldn't move. All the sound around me got fuzzy. Leaning forward, I tried to keep from crying, but the tears came raining down.

Papa's face touched mine before I even heard his feet on the stairs. "Nissa, it's all right. I'm okay."

Pulling away, I ran upstairs. I buried myself in bed. How could Mama do it? Sure, I hit Peter Roubidoux, but I hated that boy—enough to wish him harm. Mama loved Papa. What could make a person hit someone they love?

Papa's voice came to me from what seemed like far away. Then I realized I'd started to sob so loud, I couldn't hear real good. He rubbed my back, telling me, "Calm down, now. It's going to be all right."

Rolling over, I screamed, "She hit you!"

Papa poked at his puffy cheek which was turning more shades of purple than the petals on one of Mama's prized roses. "She walloped me good."

"Doesn't it hurt you? I mean, inside." I tapped my chest.

Papa nodded. "But any hurt I feel is a prick in the skin compared to how your Mama's feeling right now."

"How do you know that?"

"I know your Mama."

Sitting up, I said, "I thought I did, too. But the Mama I know would never hit someone."

"True enough." Papa rubbed my arms. "Think of it this way, she betrayed herself by hitting me. And that hurts a hell of a lot worse than a punch in the face."

I felt betrayed, too, so I knew just what Papa meant.

"Now what?" I asked.

"I go downstairs and drown myself in some cold water." Papa stood up.

"You're not mad at Mama for hitting you?"

Papa shook his head. "No. Getting angry at a time like that is how fist fights start. And you can't end your pain by making more."

Papa told the truth. Too bad Mama didn't live by the same rule.

And after Papa went downstairs, Lara had her say. Even from upstairs, I could hear Lara yelling, "We can't let her go, Ivar. That woman could hurt her."

Scrambling off the bed, I listened for Papa's response by putting my ear to the floor. He said, "That woman is her mother. Heirah would never hurt Nissa."

"Just like she wouldn't hurt you?"

"It'll never happen again."

"And you're willing to bet your child's safety on that?"

Papa didn't answer. Or at least I never heard him if he did. Truth be told, I hadn't felt safe for a long time. The moods in my family changed more often than the weather. One minute, the day is sunshiny and warm, next minute a hurricane passes through and blows all the life clean out of me. And with my family, it's not like I could buy myself an umbrella or build a storm shelter to hide in. No matter what I did or where I went, they'd find me. The best I could do was weather the storm and come out the other side with a little bit of knowing to help me live through the next squall.

And with Lara brewing over Mama's sudden violent streak, I worried that another storm waited just over the horizon. Sitting in my window, I realized part of the problem was that Papa surrounded himself with runners. Anytime I got so worked up I couldn't see straight, I'd hightail it and run. Lara stomped out after only one big fight with Papa. And Mama, well she traveled with the breeze—going out, coming in—never staying put. The only person in the family to stand in one place was Papa. He never ran off or even backed down. The man was a tree, pure and simple.

I didn't take to being a runner. In fact, I decided to plant myself in a mental kind of way. No more running for me. I'd stand my ground and face things head on. Hiding away in my brain somewhere was the idea that I didn't have the guts to stay put when another storm hit, but I sure felt dedicated to the idea at the time.

That afternoon, I packed my bags. I'd made the decision to go to Chicago and I planned to stick to it. Pulling clothes out of the closet, I began to wonder what kind of things I'd need up North. What kind of summer did they have up there? With no way of knowing, I just packed everything I had. Made things simple in the end.

"Would you shove me out if I came in through this window?" Mama startled me. I nearly went the opposite direction of my skin when I turned to find her in the window.

"What'd you go and hit Papa for?"

"For telling the truth." Mama stood in the window—half in half out—just like in my life. She was never fully there. "Lies don't hurt near as much as the truth when it's told by someone you love."

"Maybe so, but you didn't have to hit him."

"Yelling at me won't change things."

"Fine." I went back to the suitcase on my bed. Leaning all my weight on it, I snapped the clasps shut, saying, "I'm going to Chicago for two weeks. No less, no more."

"Really?" Mama stepped inside. "Why's that?"

I had no reason other than the fact I wanted to give Papa a

definite time so he wouldn't worry about me not coming back. "Seems like a good amount of time to me."

"How about 17 days or 15 and a half?"

"Stop teasing me."

Mama laughed. "I'm sorry. You just seem so stiff all of a sudden."

"I get that way when people hurt my papa."

"People?" Mama took a step back. "Who am I, the milkman?"

Mama put up a finger to hush me. "Don't answer that." Sitting on the trunk between my windows, she said, "You ever eaten a whole box of chocolates?"

"No."

"Well, I happen to know you've gobbled down an entire batch of snickerdoodles."

Mama made the best snickerdoodles. I could taste that divine mix of cinnamon, sugar, and shortbread just by hearing their name. I'd been known to eat half a dozen of them without so much as pausing for a drink of milk. "Guilty as charged."

"Well, you ever try to not eat more than one?"

"I'd be a fool to try."

"You're not making this any easier, Nissa."

"I didn't know I was supposed to be helping."

"You are!" Mama slapped the trunk. "I'm trying to tell you how it is with me."

"Then just tell me." For the life of me, I didn't know why adults always thought I needed examples to understand what they were going through. Wasn't I living near about the same life as them?

"All right." Mama stood up. "It's like this. You do one thing you promised yourself you'd never do, then somehow, your mind goes soft and you start breaking all your own rules. When you were born, I told myself I'd never leave you, but I did. And I told

God to strike me dead if I ever raised a hand to another human being except in my own defense. Luckily, God doesn't take orders from me."

I laughed, but felt heavy with the weight of knowing why Papa'd whispered in Mama's ear like he did. He knew just how Mama felt about breaking her rule about leaving me.

"It's like the walls inside me are breaking down. And I've got to find a way to build them back up."

I had an idea of what Mama was trying to tell me. It sounded like my plan of planting roots. Mama had her mind on rebuilding while I had been focusing on building, but we were working for the same things. "I understand."

"Do you?" Mama leaned toward me.

I nodded. "Near enough."

"Then you know it'd knock a hole in my heart if I ever did anything like that again?"

By the desperate look in her eyes, I figured Mama and Lara danced on the same coin. They might be dancing on different sides, but both of them wanted to be certain Mama never raised a hand to me. "I won't let you do it, Mama."

Mama bunched up her brow. "I told you, Nissa. That isn't your job. I'm the one in charge of me. It's my job to keep control."

"Right."

We stared at each other for a bit. If Mama felt like I did, she was struggling to decide if she should laugh, cry, or throw something. Then Mama said, "You packed already?"

"I want to go now."

"Before anything else goes wrong?"

I shrugged. "I guess."

"Your Papa won't let you go without a birthday party."

"I don't need one."

"Oh really?" Mama stood up. "Then I guess you don't want cake or presents."

"No ma'am."

"How about a birthday tickle?"

"No," I shook my head and started skirting around the bed, but Mama had me in the wink of an eye. Holding me down, she tickled me until I near about burst a lung. Still leaning on me, Mama stopped to catch her breath, saying, "Oh I wish I could bottle that laugh."

"Huh." I squirmed, but couldn't get loose "Mary Carroll says my laugh sounds like a hundred marbles being scrambled up in a jar."

"And I'd agree." Mama kissed me on the cheek, then got up.

"Can we go soon, Mama?"

"Not so fast, quicksilver." Mama stood up. "I need to make my peace with your papa." She headed for the door, then said over her shoulder, "Not to mention that small matter of a birthday party you seem to be avoiding."

Homeleaving

Turns out that Papa didn't take to the idea of me leaving early and Mr. Carroll wanted all the time he could get with his family. Can't say as I blame him for that. But I couldn't agree with him on all counts, especially when his staying meant I had to spend a week with my whole family: Lara giving Mama the evil stare every time she came into the room; Papa walking around with a black and blue reminder of Mama's crumbling rules. And I had to keep digging into my already-packed suitcase to get dressed every day.

Not to mention the not-so-secret attempts to plan my birthday party—the ribbon streamers I saw Lara stuffing under the sink, the invitations Papa wasn't writing when I came into his study to bring him a glass of tea, and the odd giggle Mary seemed to be infected with every time she came over.

Getting older isn't as grand as everybody makes it out to be. Sure you can do things like get married, start a family, and vote, but who wants to do any of those things when they go right along with working every day, worrying about bill paying, child rearing, and keeping your house from falling down with repairs and such. Adulthood—no thank you. It could go right down the same river with marriage as far as I was concerned.

I figured my party would be in my house, so I conveniently went out for a walk that morning. When I got home, the house stood empty. The doors and windows hung wide open like the people inside might be enjoying the breeze, but everything stood quiet and still.

Going out the back door, I called out for Mama who didn't answer, so I tried for Papa, then Lara, even Mary, but no one yelled back. I thought they were hiding in the alley, so I shouted, "All right you all, I know you're hiding. Come out with your surprise!"

Silence. Opening the back gate, I saw rose petals on the ground. Looking back, I saw that Mama's rose bushes were bare. That sight still haunted me from when she harvested them before walking out of our lives two springs before. I realized that the sprinkling of rose petals went clear down the alley. Running that way, I saw that they led the way up the bank to the railroad tracks. Dorothy could have her yellow bricks, I'd take my path of rose petals any day.

The petals went straight to the back door of the Crocked Gator. The porch stood ready for the evening dinner crowd, but nobody was there. Stepping in the door, I expected to be greeted by a group whooping, "Surprise!"

They stumped me again. Not a soul inside. Running out the front door, I found nobody, then something tapped me on the head, followed by another, then another. Leaning back I stared up into a rainfall of rose petals to the tune of "Happy Birthday to You!" Mama sang as I laughed.

People came rushing out of the bushes, from under the front porch, the nearby houses, and parked cars all singing and shouting, "Happy Birthday to You!"

I turned into a giggling mess of happiness all laughing and crying at the same time. Papa hugged me and kissed me on the top of my head. He came away with a rose petal stuck to his lips. I near about peed my britches laughing at him talking away like there was nothing there.

That night we ate crawfish patties instead of cake, had enough watermelon to send us floating down a river—danced, laughed, and carried on until the fireflies came to light up our party. By that time, we'd all sprawled out on the grass to share stories.

Mr. Dupree told us how he and his brothers tried to take a raft down the Amite River like Jim and Huck only to end up wedged on a row of rocks surrounded by a herd of cows too hot to stay in the field and too stupid not to stand so close together they choked on one another's body heat. Old Otis finished his story by saying, "That's the last time I take a nap at sea!" Everyone laughed.

"Now, Miss Nissa," Ira shouted from across the way. "You'll have to tell us how they treat our kind up there in Chicago."

"That's right," Ira's brother Leo added. "Ira and I've got cousins who went up there looking to get some respect."

"Respect?" Otis laughed. "Hell, they'll be happy if they get themselves a job."

Everyone laughed again, but this time the laughter had a hard edge to it. People always said folks treated black people better up North.

People started talking amongst themselves, then Lara, putting down her fifth piece of watermelon, piped up saying, "I've got a story."

Everyone stared at her. As a newcomer who never set foot in the cafe before she married Papa, folks were suspicious of her color, if you know what I mean. You never know if folks can leave their color at the door or not. Lara must have felt all the stares because she looked kind of red in the face, but she told her story anyhow. "When I was Nissa's age, or a bit younger, I suppose, my sister and I decided we could act. Not that we ever did more than stutter our way through a few lines in the annual Christmas pageant, but we were convinced we had what it takes to light up a stage."

"What'd you do, Miss Lara?" Rinnie Lee asked. "Make your way to Hollywood?"

"We tried." Lara laughed. "Saved up our baby-sitting money for months, but the closest we could get to California was Kansas City."

"Kansas City!" Ira shouted. "You could do musicals for the cows!

"Nawh, that's Otis's gig!" Leo shouted back.

Everyone laughed. Lara listened nervously, not so much as parting her lips, then Mrs. Villeneuve gave her a nudge, saying, "Go on, dear."

"Well, you were almost right, Ira. We made it to Kansas City and thought we could train hop the rest of the way. But we got caught on the first train we tried to hop. Jumped right up into the break car. Walked in on a table full of railroad workers playing gin rummy."

Everyone laughed as I tried to imagine Lara and her older sister Kate standing there in a train car staring at a bunch of coal-coated men playing cards. Or maybe they were conductor types in blue uniforms with the shiny brass buttons. Either way it would've been enough to make me want to melt into the floor.

"Then what?" Rinnie Lee asked.

"They wired my father who insisted on sending us home freight. He told the men at the station to ship us back with the other ham bones. Didn't know what he meant until they locked us in the pig car. Stunk so bad, I thought I'd die."

Otis Dupree shook his head as the rest of the folks howled with laughter, even Mama who slapped her knee and swayed from left to right trying to get air.

"Speaking of smelling!" Rinnie Lee piped up from her perch on the arm of Ira's chair. "I remember the first time I met Miss Heirah over there." She waved a hand in Mama's direction. Mama just laughed, but most of the other folks were ohhing like Rinnie Lee was about to let a secret out of the bag.

"Do tell!" Otis shouted.

For the first time that night, I started to study people's faces—the way Ira watched Rinne Lee like she was a movie star up on the screen. And Otis closed his eyes and tapped his foot when he listened to a good story. Lara had her arm laced through Papa's and she had a dreamy look on her face as if she was only half there. Mama kept her eyes on Rinnie Lee, an "I remember that" look on her face—half happiness, half wishful thinking.

Closing my eyes, I leaned up against Papa and let the information my ears brought in fill my head with the images of a memory I could only share from the distance and nostalgia all good storytelling brings.

"I sat on the porch out back skinning potatoes out to a trio of coons. The evening was going black. All of the sudden I get hit by this smell like a cloud full of flowers hanging over me raining out pollen. I turned and there stood this white woman as pale as the moon, saying, 'Mind if I have a glass a water?'

"I'm staring at her thinking she's out of her mind walking up to my place in the dark smelling like a bee's ass." Everyone laughed, including Mama.

"So, I says, 'Sure, I'll go right in and get that.' And I did.

"When I came out, Heirah had them coons turning in circles to get the peelings. Dropping a peeling down, she took the glass of water from me, then said, 'You should think of putting a bucket of water out there for them. You know how those critters love to wash their food before they eat.'

"Drinking that water down, she handed the glass back saying, 'Thank you very much,' then disappeared up the tracks. I stood there thinking I'd either seen a ghost or been visited by Demeter herself!"

"Demeter!" Mama screeched with laughter. "You've got to be kidding me."

"Well, I learned better later," Rinnie Lee teased.

People kept talking as I lay back in the grass and watched the stars blinking into view as the sky went black. Some folks have a homecoming, but I couldn't escape the feeling that the folks around me were telling stories so I had part of home to take with me. I think I had Harper's first "homeleaving" party. And it made me feel just fine.

Chicken Crates
and Fire Escapes

Our trip North started with a game of musical cars. Papa gave
our old Tin Lizzie to Mrs. Carroll, and Mama and I loaded all our
things into the Carrolls' old truck. When it came time to go, Mrs.
Carroll tried to make everything go smoothly, saying in a real
calm voice, "You have a safe trip now, Jacob."

It didn't matter, though; Mary and April started crying. Even
Little Anthony looked like his eyes were about to spring a leak.
The Carrolls got to hugging and making vows about writing
every day.

On our side of the truck, I felt like I was eavesdropping again.
Papa kept rearranging my collar and saying, "I'll be seeing you
soon." I smiled and nodded my head, hoping he'd stop. I didn't
like the pulling feeling in my heart. I wanted to just get on the
road and make it stop.

Lara gave me a quick, stiff hug, saying, "I'm sorry we didn't
have more time to say good-bye." I don't know what she was
talking about. We had two weeks. By the looks of her, she'd been
too busy eating. Her nervous habit was beginning to show.

I turned to climb up into the truck, but Papa spun me around and gave me a hug that could have squeezed the air out of a bear. "I'll be missing you."

Mama said, "She'll be dead if you don't let go."

Papa laughed, then stood back, his eyes all misty. He mouthed the words, "Love you, Neesay."

I knew I'd cry if I didn't get in that truck in a hurry, so I scrambled up into the seat. Slamming the door shut, I waved frantically, praying Mr Carroll would get himself in the truck and start it up right quick. "Bye!" I shouted as we finally pulled away.

To my surprise, I had a hard time breathing as we headed out of town. I'd driven that way a hundred times, but I had to lie and tell myself we were only going on a picnic to keep from hyper-ventilating. Made me see what a small town girl I really was. Even the fear of leaving home sent me over the edge.

When Mama did her share of the driving, Mr. Carroll sat by the door and slept. Funny thing was, he looked just like Mary when she fell asleep during history lessons, which happened far too often. That's when Mama took to travelling in a whole new fashion. Coming to a pig farm, Mama stopped the truck so we could get out and scratch a pig's back for good luck. At the parks along the roadside, Mama and I'd get out and chase out the fatigue in our bones. We'd pick apples in orchards, leave money in the crook of the tree, then feed the fruit to horses miles and miles away. Catching sight of a field of water-melon, Mama jumped out of the truck, scooped up a melon, pulled out a pocket knife, and cut each of us a slice. Climbing back over the fence, Mama left a nickel behind on the post. Wrapping the melon in a towel, we had a ready-made treat for quite a ways. Mama'd collected a fine assortment of travelling activities that made the whole trip slip on by.

The state of Illinois looked like a steamrolled, giant-sized, well-cooked pie crust—all flat and brown. Why would anybody build one of the world's largest cities in such an ugly place?

Buffalo was the biggest city I'd ever seen, but the places we went weren't anything like Chicago. Sure the houses stood close enough together for neighbors to be able to borrow a cup of sugar without leaving their kitchens, but I never saw the packed-in, sky-itching buildings like they have in Chicago. A person could get dizzy just looking up to the top of one of those things. There were more cars on the street with us, honking and switching lanes like they were in a race, than in the fields around the Tucumsett Parish Fair on opening day. And the people? I saw more folks in one block than I might see in a week back home. Seemed like God had taken an entire state, then cinched it up into a tiny little plot of land—crowding in every little thing until there was barely room enough to breathe.

I thought I might just faint straight away until Mama pulled out onto a road that overlooked a body of water so big it could've been an ocean.

"Lake Michigan," Mama announced.

"That's just a lake?"

"That's right."

"You could sink a pirate ship in there and never find it."

Mama laughed, but Mr. Carroll was caught up in an open-mouthed stare just like me. The lakes I knew had a shoreline you could see from either side on a clear day. All I saw of the other shore of Lake Michigan were blue waves and clouds. At least all those city folks had something natural to look at instead of just brick, glass, and steel.

It was a good thing Mama drove into the city because Mr. Carroll just kept staring out the window, saying, "I don't think I'm going to like it here."

I agreed with him. As we turned a corner, we saw a line of

people longer than the one for getting into the livestock exhibits at the fair—all men, looking tired and worn out.

"A job line," Mama said. "That factory there hires some of their workers by the day."

"They're waiting in line for a job?" I asked as we passed them by.

"There's maybe ten jobs in one day." Mama shook her head.

"And I'm taking a job from some man who lives in this city?" Mr. Carroll looked like Mama had just told him he'd caused somebody to die.

"Don't think of it that way," Mama said. "Folks come streaming into the city every day from all over. Jobs are tight everywhere. You take what you can get."

"I don't feel right about it."

Mama shifted gears, saying, "You'll feel just fine when you send that first check home to Patricia and the kids." She turned the truck and went dipping down into what looked like a cave.

"Mama, what's this?"

"It's for parking, Nissa." We drove down into a long, low room like a warehouse with pillars all over the place and cars parked between them.

"Parking under a building?"

"Better than on top of it," Mama said, pulling in next to a black car.

She had a point there. Getting to the top of buildings was no picnic. Leaving the luggage in the car, we went into a cage fit for animals. They called it an elevator.

"So they have you on duty today, Miss Eleanor," Mama said to an older lady hanging onto what looked like the gearshift of a tractor sticking out of the wall.

"That's right, Heirah Rae. Where to?"

"Heading for the lobby."

"Here we go." Eleanor gave the gear a yank and the cage went screeching and crawling up the inside of the building like some steel tapeworm headed for the belly.

Mama tried to introduce me, and Miss Eleanor seemed nice enough, but that cage made me nervous. I just nodded in her direction.

"Have a good day, Miss Eleanor," Mama said as she yanked open the gate. I jumped out right quick. She led the way down a long hallway lined with doors, saying, "We can't afford an elevator man so we take turns operating it."

I prayed I'd never have to take a turn as Mama went on, saying, "Back in the days when fools thought money fell from the sky, this was a big fancy hotel. They closed it down in 1930. Sat empty for five years, then Mr. Keller borrowed some money to turn it into apartments and a theater." Facing us, she said, "What else are you going to do with a dining room that seats three hundred?"

Three hundred people sitting down to one meal? You'd need a dozen cooks to feed all those people. And I pitied the folks who had to clean up after all that. Their hands would've turned to prunes after doing all those dishes.

"Here we are." Mama pushed her way through doors made of glass. I'd never seen such a thing. Who would ever think to stick two windows on hinges and walk right through them? These windows didn't have wooden frames; they were surrounded by shiny silver. Four more just like it led out onto the street. People walked by like they saw such things every day. I suppose they did.

The floor under my feet was carpeted. Not the rugs people throw around to soak up all the dust from your wood floor and cut down on the noise, but real, stapled-to-the-floor carpet. I felt like shucking off my shoes to dig in my toes. The room we stood in had a long wooden counter with a wall of mail cubbyholes behind it—the old check-in desk, I gathered. Struck still by the chandelier, I realized there was enough glass in that thing to make a window the size of a wall. I'd seen pictures of chandeliers, even saw the real thing in Eloise Simpson's house, but nothing like that one. The darn thing could blind someone.

"Come on, Nissa. I want you to meet Mr. Keller." Mama pulled me into an office kind of like Papa's study, but there were piles of papers on the shelves instead of books.

A man behind the desk in a funny kind of button-up sweater saw Mama and he near about jumped to the ceiling with excitement. "Heirah Rae! My angel. We were about to send enough train tickets for your entire crew if you didn't hurry back."

"Train tickets, my big toe. You couldn't afford a ticket for the city bus."

The man's smile twisted into a frown. He nodded his head at Mr. Carroll, "Watch what you say."

"I never have, Tom, and I don't plan to start now." Putting her hand on my shoulder, Mama said, "Here's my girl. Nissa Bergen, this is Thomas Keller, founder, proprietor, and director of the Sunburst Theater Company."

Mr. Keller still seemed sour about Mama talking money, but he offered his hand to me. I shook it, thinking how much it felt like mashed potatoes in a leather glove. "Welcome, Nissa."

"Thank you, Mr. Keller."

He stepped past me, then offered a hand to Mr. Carroll. "You must be Jacob."

"Yes, sir." Mr. Carroll nodded.

"We'll let Heirah show her daughter to their apartment and you and I will take a tour of the place."

I got a charge of excitement when he said "their apartment," partly because I'd finally get to see where Mama lived, but mostly because it meant her home was my home. Unfortunately, we had to ride up to the apartment in that elevator cage.

"Aren't there stairs?" I asked Mama. Miss Eleanor snickered.

"Twelve flights of them."

"Anything would be better than this thing."

"You say that now. Wait until it breaks down and you have to use the stairs."

By the time we reached the fourteenth floor I was ready to fly upstairs if it meant no more elevators. Waiting for Mama to open the cage, I realized something. "Mama?"

"Yes."

"Didn't we start on the first floor and come up twelve flights?"

"That's right."

"Then how come it says fourteen?" I pointed at the number above the cage door.

Miss Eleanor piped in saying, "Folks around here are so superstitious, they don't make a thirteenth floor."

"You don't say," I said, stepping into the hall. People in cities rode in cages and feared the number thirteen. "Folks around here are nuts."

Opening her apartment door for me, Mama said, "You've sure got that right."

I can't imagine why, but as the door opened, I expected to see flowers—an indoor garden, I guess. What I did see looked more like a larger version of Mama's keeping room. Turns out Mama didn't lose that treasure trove after all.

The room we entered could have been a parlor if space had been made for a chair or a couch. Instead, various odds and ends cluttered the space—a sewing machine covered with heaps of fabric in shades of brown, blue, and red; panels of half-painted canvas as tall as a screen door and twice as wide; and the only plants around were those made out of paper and painted to look real.

Mama walked right on through the mess and into the kitchen

to open a window, saying, "Don't mind the prop room, Nissa. I made your bedroom up nice. It's to the left."

Seeing a closed door I hoped would rescue me from that jumbled mess, I headed across the room. Then I noticed the walls in the parlor prop room. Dotted all over the surface of the dingy gray walls were tiny half-done drawings of castle walls, tropical sunsets, stormy seascapes, and craggy mountains. The tiny drawings looked like murals Mama didn't have the heart to finish. They made me wonder if some part of Mama had started to shrink.

Peeking into the room next to mine, I saw that clothing hung like kudzu all over, off the mirror across the vanity, on the chair by the unmade bed, sticking out of the dresser, in mounds around the room. The place looked like the burrow of a wild animal that made a nest out of human clothing. My mama lived like this?

I opened the door fully intent on hiding there until it was time to go back to Harper. The shades had been drawn, so the room had a half-dark look. Crossing to the window, I sent a shade swirling up, then nearly fell down. The drop outside my window was enough to send my stomach up with the shade. How could people live in a city? All packed together like chickens going to a slaughterhouse, one crate stacked on top of another, every hen clucking so loud you can't hear anything else for miles.

Turning around, I guessed at an answer. City folk fooled themselves into believing they lived somewhere else. Mama had painted bricks on my walls. Flowers streamed down from the ceiling, telling me there was a beautiful garden just beyond the walls. Along the floorboards, Mama had painted little animals nibbling at the tips of the flowery vines hanging down. Closing my eyes, I could almost hear the rabbit nibbling away on a wisteria.

Mama'd covered my bed with a quilt of blossoming rosebuds in every color. The floor didn't have so much as a dust mouse. The washstand had white linen towels and a berry blue pitcher and basin. The dresser had been carved into a bookshelf. It still had plenty of hiding space for clothes, but the front of every drawer looked like a shelf crammed full of books. That room could have been hidden inside our house in Harper my whole life.

Mama opened the door. Having the good sense God gave her, she closed it behind her to keep the chaos in the parlor from seeping into my room. Leaning against the door, Mama said, "What do you think?"

Hoping Mama was referring only to my room, I said, "Looks like you pulled it straight out of our house."

"Sorry about the blue spot on your yellow rose." Mama tapped a sky blue petal in a yellow rosebud with her foot. "I ran out of yellow fabric."

"You sewed this?" I asked, rushing forward to put my hand on it. The only thing I'd ever seen Mama sew was the occasional rip.

"Just because I never chose to sew doesn't mean I don't know how." Mama smiled and I wondered what else she knew how to do.

Walking over to the dresser, she rubbed the top, saying, "I thought this here would remind you of your Papa."

It did. "Shouldn't I give him a call?"

"Right you are." Mama went back to the door. "I'll go down and get our luggage. You go to Mr. Keller's office and call your Papa."

As we came out onto the first floor, I thought how easy it would be to get lost. That place made me think of a forest of young trees, every one the same and no ground markings to show you the way. I passed door after door, each one as plain and gray as the last. I began to wonder if folks didn't sometimes go to the wrong door by mistake. The only thing that set that floor apart from the one I'd left was the grand room with the glass doors. The office was empty, so I went right in. Picking up the phone, I looked for the crank to put a charge through, but there was no handle, only a dial. *Now what?* I thought, staring at the phone.

"You trying to work that thing with the power of your mind?"

I jumped around to see Mr. Keller standing in the doorway.

"How do you get an operator?"

"You dial zero," he said, sounding like I'd asked him what you got when you put two and two together. "What do you do back home? Send up a flag?"

I chose to ignore him, knowing it was never good to anger one of Mama's bosses. She did a good enough job of that on her own. Picking up the phone, I dialed the operator.

"I'd like Harper, Louisiana, please."

"My, don't you have a sweet little southern voice," the operator said back to me. In my way of thinking her words sounded like they were stomped on before she let them out of her mouth—all flat and ugly.

"Harper, Louisiana," I repeated.

"I heard you the first time, dear."

Pretty soon, I heard Becky's voice say, "Harper." And it made me feel like I stood a world away from home.

"Becky!" I shouted. "This is Nissa Bergen. I need to speak to Papa."

"Nissa? Girl, you calling from Chicago?"

"Yes, ma'am."

"What's it like up there?"

"Big. Can you send me over to the Minkies'?"

"I'll do you one better. I'll go get your Papa from here. He's only a few doors down and you won't have half the folks in Harper listening in."

"Thank you, Becky."

"Sure thing. Anytime you need a little bit to throw back at that Chessie Roubidoux, you just tell me. I've heard every phone conversation that backbiting woman's ever had and she deserves a bit of her own medicine."

"Thanks, Becky."

I heard a click, then Becky was gone. A few minutes later, Papa came on the line, panting, "Neesay?"

"Papa!" Facing the wall to keep Mr. Keller out of my business, I said, "It's just awful."

"What do you mean? Were you in an accident?"

"No, Papa. I'm fine. Mama's house."

"What about it?"

"A pig would refuse to live there. It's so messy."

"Your Mama's never been known for her housekeeping, Nissa."

"The only flowers are the ones she painted on my bedroom walls."

"That sounds lovely."

"Papa, you're not listening." I wanted him to know that Mama had left Harper because she didn't feel at home, then moved into the worst place on earth only to build a secret part of our home out of a dingy gray, chicken crate of an apartment.

Papa said, "I'm listening, Nissa, and it sounds to me like you're looking at your Mama through somebody else's eyes."

I tried to protest, but I recognized the tint of Chessie in my voice.

"You give your mama time. She'll reveal her reasons."

"For living like a pig?"

"Nissa," Papa warned.

"Yes, Papa."

"Go on now, your mama's probably got a lot to show you."

If those things looked anything like her apartment, I didn't want to see them, but I said, "Yes, Papa."

"I love you, Neesay."

"I love you, too, Papa."

"Give my best to Heirah."

"I will. Bye."

"See you soon."

Hanging up the phone, I wished that soon was tomorrow, then I went upstairs to face the pigsty Mama called home.

I heard the clanking of dishes as I came in. Mama stood in a closet of a kitchen washing the dishes. If I lay down on the floor in that room, my fingers would touch the wall under the window and my feet would stick out the door.

"I guess city folks don't cook much," I said.

"I throw what I can think of into a pan, cook it until it's mushy, then nibble on it for a week," Mama said, rubbing a glass bowl clean.

My stomach tucked itself in at the thought of eating such things.

"Oh, don't give me such a sour face." Mama flicked suds at me. "Sometimes it's good. Sometimes, I feed it to the pigeons on the roof."

"You've got pigeons?"

"Everyone in the city does. Whether they want them or not."

I'd heard pigeons ate right out of people's hands. I'd never had a bird so much as land within ten feet of me. Except maybe those courting birds who flew through the house. They got pretty close, but didn't take no heed of me. I was just thinking how nice it would be to have a bird pecking a meal out of my hand when somebody came bursting through the door.

"Heirah Rae?" shouted this woman who looked like she'd just as soon flap her arms than take a plane because she'd get there faster. "Have you got the fairy costumes?"

"Darla, meet my girl, Nissa," Mama said, nodding to me as she wiped her hands on her apron.

"Nice to meet you." Darla gave me a quick look, then said to Mama, "The costumes, Heirah? We only have three days. I have to have them fitted."

And before Darla could take a breath to say the next thing, Mama jumped right in and said it with her, word for word, "We wouldn't want fairies with saggy britches, now, would we."

Darla stood still for the first time. In an instant, she realized Mama just might be mocking her. Putting her hands on her hips, she said, "Now, Heirah!"

"Yes, Darla?" Mama asked, going to a closet to take out a handful of costumes on hangers. All gauzy and sparkly, they had to be fairy clothes, although Mama always said she favored a hearty Celtic fairy who rode a horse and lived in a hill to any old flittery, firefly of a sprite that goes hopping around flowers all day.

"I need those . . ." Seeing the costumes, Darla stopped. "Costumes."

"And they're already fitted, Darla. The fairy crew came up to make a batch of pixie dust out of the leftover fabric, so I thought I'd take the opportunity."

"That's my job, Heirah. Are you trying—"

Mama cut her off, saying, "I'm trying to put on the best show we can. You've got your hands full designing the programs and keeping the playwrights happy." She handed over the costumes.

I don't know how she does it, but Mama can twist people around so fast they act like a bird that's flown into a closed window. Darla came in all rush and bother, then left slow and stunned.

"Darla did all the costumes until someone found out I could sew."

"How'd they find out?"

"I wanted a new dress and didn't have the money for it, so I bought some curtains at a secondhand store and sewed them into a dress."

"Curtains?" I laughed.

"Be still your chattering teeth," Mama said, heading for her bedroom. "I think it's mighty nice."

"And you think you can find it in here?" I asked, standing in the bedroom doorway.

"Organization by tornado. You don't like it?" Mama tried to look serious, but we both started laughing. Going to the closet, she pulled out a pale green dress with a full skirt, ruffles for sleeves, and a long, plain front perfect for a string of pearls to hang down over.

"It's a beaut."

"No more laughing then." Mama shook the dress in the air like it was dancing by itself. "I lined it with an old sheet, so it doesn't itch when I wear it.

"Lets have ourselves a slice of sky before we settle in for the night," Mama said, stomping on her own clothes to go over to the window. City windows are small, high off the ground, and made funny. You have to push one square window up over another one to open them. Back home, most windows had two multi-paned sections that opened outward, and they were big, like doors. Only a few feet off the floor, you could step right out of them if you had a mind to. This one you had to crawl out of like some crazed thief in reverse.

Outside Mama's window hung a rusty metal landing with an old staircase leading up to the top of the building and another going down toward the street below. Mama called it a fire escape which made me wonder about the safety of the folks in the building next door. They didn't even have a single window facing the alley, let alone a fire escape. The brick was as black as coal dust.

Trash lined the alley below. The only good thing about the view was that the building next door stood only twelve stories, so we could see over the roof to the night sky.

"Now you see why I wanted to live up here." Mama leaned over the railing, her arms out to her sides, and took a deep breath.

City air smelled like poison to me. I'd already caught myself holding my breath once or twice.

"This summer, I'm going to get some flowers out here. Maybe even put in a garden on the roof."

"With the pigeons." I liked the idea. Made me want to get started right away.

Mama stared up at the sky. "What I do when I long for the open spaces of home is take a piece of the sky with me to bed."

"What?"

"I pick my own piece full of stars. And close my eyes. Then hold it in my head all night. Makes me feel free." Mama closed her eyes and smiled.

I thought of taking my own sky view to bed, but it didn't seem right to snatch any from Mama. I felt happy enough just seeing her staring into her own head, enjoying the night sky. Walking over, I leaned against her. Wrapping her arms around me, she made me feel like I just might like Chicago after all.

The New Mama

Sleeping proved to be quite a challenge in my room-sized home away from home. The sounds drifting in through the windows would've pulled a hibernating bear out of its slumber—people motoring along in their cars, honking horns, slamming doors, shouting at each other. And this god-awful sound that made me think someone was trying to strangle a goose the size of a house over and over again pulled me right out of bed. At the window, I found out that's what a siren sounds like in the middle of the night when I saw a police car zoom down the street below.

Back in Harper, the only siren we've got is Chessie Roubidoux running into the streets shouting, "There's a fire down at the old Miller place! There's a fire!"

I would've paid part of my big toe for the quiet of Harper where the loudest noise you hear are the cicadas electrocuting the night. Of course, some nights, if I listened real close, I could hear the music from the Crocked Gator drifting in from a distance far enough away to pull the sass down to a minimum and leave the notes lazy and soothing. If only I could convince my brain all that city racket carried a tune.

I had no such luck. Instead, I twisted and turned my way through the night, until Mama came bounding into the room. I wanted to throw rocks at her, but she jumped on my bed, and started kissing me all over and tickling me, saying, "Morning, morning, morning" like some crazed bird.

In spite of my sour mood, I started laughing.

"I won't even ask how you slept," Mama said, giving me one final kiss on the forehead before she stood up. "I'll just treat you to breakfast with my apologies."

"Treat me?" I hadn't heard that phrase before.

"That means I'll buy you breakfast at The Silver Spoon."

"What's that?" I asked, suspecting Mama had named her own closet of a kitchen.

"The coffee shop on the first floor."

"We're going to have breakfast in a restaurant?" I hopped out of bed like I was still eight, the age I'd been when Papa'd suggested the same idea while we were in Buffalo.

"I'm afraid that's the only way you'll get breakfast around here." Mama walked out the door. "I don't cook before noon."

Wriggling into my clothes, I came out into the prop room. I could see from the shine in the paint on the canvas in the middle of the room that Mama had already been working. Checking the clock in the kitchen, I saw that it was only 8:30 in the morning.

"You may not cook before noon, but you sure do get up early."

"It's quiet." I stared at Mama, thinking the city never shut up as far as I could tell. She laughed, saying, "Well, there's only a dull roar after dawn."

"Dawn?"

"Nothing like a sunrise to get your fingers itching to paint." Mama scrunched up her fingers like claws.

From the looks of the canvas, she scratched that itch pretty good. Her doorway of a castle looked so real, I wanted to walk in and find out just what they served in the dining room I could see in the distance. In the end, I had to settle for what they served in the coffee shop.

All I remembered of the cafe we'd gone to in Buffalo were shiny Formica counters and spongy blueberry pancakes with pecan syrup and watery-tasting milk. The Silver Spoon had swivel seats, high-back booths with gray vinyl covers that squeaked when people slid in and out. The floor looked like a factory-made hopscotch board with its black and white tiles. And that place kept as busy as the street outside, folks coming in with a thermos for coffee on the run, men stopping in for toast and a peek at the paper before work, and women showing up with a package or two tied up in string.

The clatter of dishes bouncing around with the chattering of folks sounded like a chicken coop, but I liked it somehow. The man who sat by the window drinking orange juice and scribbling in a notebook paid no mind to the lady just a table away reading the newspaper or at least using it to catch the crumbs from the doughnut she ate. Strangers when they walked in, they'd be strangers when they left. I liked that idea. And something told me they could sit like that for a month of Sundays and never so much as say hello.

"What'll you have, Nissa?" Mama asked, tapping the menu in front of me.

I scanned the menu. The waitress who came to take our order knew Mama by name and when she said, "Morning, Heirah Rae," the smile on her face lit up her eyes. The lady really liked Mama, so I liked her.

"On behalf of the ladies in 11A, I thank you for bringing Mr. Carroll up from Louisiana," the waitress said. "He fixed our toilet in a flash."

"I'm glad." Mama put her hand over mine. "This here is my girl, Nissa."

"Aren't you just a photograph of your mother." Sure if you shrunk her down to my height, turned her eyes green, flattened her chest, then added a few pounds—we'd be twins. The comment always made me testy. I can't say why.

I just smiled.

"This is Glenda. She lives with two of the other waitresses—Penny and Lisa May."

"Lisa May's southern like you. She's from Tennessee."

Tennessee's about as much like Louisiana as a fox is like a black bear, but I didn't feel like telling Glenda that, "I hope she likes the city."

"She loves it."

"I'd like some French toast and orange juice, please."

"Oh, sure." Glenda acted like I'd insulted the food before it came. Taking Mama's order, she left.

"What happened there?" Mama asked.

"What?"

"Glenda was trying to talk to you."

"Oh, I thought she was just chatting to chat."

"Uh-huh. You never were good with small talk. You must get that from me." Mama was right. She's the one who told me that nothing you do's going to change the weather, so there's no need to talk about it.

The French toast had just the right pinch of cinnamon and vanilla, but they must have done the same sort of pinching with the oranges instead of squeezing them. My juice could have gone straight through a strainer without leaving a trace.

As we finished breakfast, Darla came into the cafe all clicky heels and swinging walk. A lady behind the counter saw old Darla coming and had a tray of food ready for her.

"The hot-to-trots are having a meeting this morning," Mama said as Darla left.

"Hot-to-trots?"

"Mr. Keller and his lot. They're working on a new play as well as pushing forward on the one that opens in a few days."

"The one with the fairies."

"That's right." Mama dipped into her pocket and pulled out a coin purse. I'd never known Mama to keep a wallet. She always had her money in a kitchen drawer and fished it out when she needed some.

Mama went to the counter to pay. The man sitting next to the register looked Mama up and down like she was covered in mud that was about to drip in his coffee.

"Why's he so surly?" I nodded toward the man as Mama came back.

"Doesn't like women in britches, I suppose." Mama laughed. "Had a woman stop me on the street the other day and say"— Mama raised her voice into a squeaky imitation—"'Young lady, it's a sin to take on the airs of a man.'"

"What'd you say to her?" I asked, leaning over the table, excited to be part of Mama's escapades again.

"Well, then ma'am, I'll have to avoid that, won't I?" Mama smiled, adding, "Then I walked off."

Indeed. Hearing Mama tell her stories of daily battle gave me a charge. Like cranking up an engine to get it started, Mama's stories got me all fired up to go do things. I practically ran out of that coffee shop into the street. I slowed down quite a bit when I got there, though. The buildings towering over me made me feel closed in, then I started thinking of how many people lived behind those windows—story after story of windows. Heavens, that's a lot of people.

And the library Mama took me to probably had a book for

every one of them. The grand height of the shelves made it necessary to have ladders on wheels to get to the books on the top. The rows of books went on for so long, the last rows looked slanted to the eye. Sprinkled here or there were tables and chairs to give folks a place to sit and study. The place was large enough to carry an echo for an hour, but quiet enough to be a church on Sunday during a prayer. And it wasn't empty either. People filled the place—searching, reading, and scribbling on paper. I couldn't help wondering what all those folks discovered in those books. I had a sudden urge to read every darn one of them, but I'd have to live longer than Methuselah to get that done.

Mama patted me on the back, saying, "You wander and take it all in. I'll meet you in the 940s."

"Huh?" I asked, pulling myself out of a staring trance.

"The 940s," Mama said, tapping the spine of a book with a little number pointed on it. "They shelve the books according to subject by all these numbers. Pretty smart, don't you think?"

Mama disappeared down an aisle of books, leaving me to think she'd changed quite a bit—looking into how books are organized, spending her time in libraries, turning a parlor into a prop room, using the walls for painting practice instead of murals, leaving the housework for brownies, and eating in restaurants. Was this the life Mama always wanted? Maybe so, but it suited me about as well as wearing two left shoes.

Not the library part, mind you. I could live with a library in town. Truth be told, I'd spend a lot of my life in a library if anybody in Harper would think to build one. Coming to the end of the aisle, I found a strange sort of staircase that turned around a thick pole. As I started climbing, I felt like I might meet myself coming around. On the second floor I went up one aisle, then down another, and got lost in the idea of starting my own library.

Dreaming of the shelves and all the folks cracking the spines of books to jump into another world, I could see myself sitting at a desk, writing down who checked out what. Or I might recommend certain books for specific folks. Chessie'd probably drool over books about the kings and queens of Europe with all their high-flying morals and nasty deeds. The kids at school might even come to me for a good book to read when the rains came.

I had myself ordering books out of the catalog the Minkies kept on the dry goods counter, when I stumbled over a problem. Where would such a library go in Harper? Papa's study was full to bursting with books and who would want a public library in their house? All the buildings along Main Street had a use already. The feed store, the mercantile, the hotel, and the post office—each one of them used up every inch of space they had. Becky had to spend her days wedged into a hotel closet on account of the fact Mr. Cassell couldn't offer her any more room.

Sitting down on a windowsill, I started a mental walk through Harper trying to find a place to put my library. Walking out of town, it hit me. Lara's house. The place stood empty. That was it! I could use Lara's house—fill every room with bookshelves, ask folks to donate books, and build up our own little collection. Papa's donations would fill up a whole room, maybe two. And Papa had himself a regular source for new books like a literary river flowing into his pond of a study. A fella named Vernon Finch, who ran a used bookstore in Baton Rouge, sent Papa a box of books every month or so in exchange for advertisements Papa printed up then sent down. Mr. Finch would be a monthly contributor. I'd have myself a regular library in no time at all. What a grand idea. I went in search of Mama to tell her so.

Watching the numbers as I walked by, I found my way to the 900s. Turning a corner, I found Mama. The floor around her was scattered with open books, Mama sprawled out among them, reading away. Laughing, I realized Mama hadn't changed that much after all, looking like she did when she read the Sunday paper.

"Nissa," Mama said in a shouted whisper, "there's a city with your name."

"Really?" I asked, getting down to Mama's level. "Where?"

"Macedonia."

"Where'd the devil put that?"

"It's curled around the top of the Aegean Sea like a hat," Mama said, running a finger along a map in the book she was reading.

We'd studied the Aegean Sea in school—the stomping grounds of Alexander the Great, as Mrs. Owens called it. "Really?"

"But the darn fools smooshed the name down to Nis a few hundred years ago. Now it's just a boring old city in Yugoslavia. I always thought the name was all Norwegian."

Seemed kind of strange to have two cities with my name. There's Bergen, Norway, and Nissa, Macedonia. And here I was a girl from Louisiana who could barely find those two places on a map. "Why you studying all this?"

"For a play. Mr. Keller brought in this history professor who wrote a play about the people's crusade before the first knights' crusade."

"What?" I laughed, hearing Mama talk about crusades like she knew what they were. One time, I came running downstairs all fired up about the Japanese warriors I read about in a book of Papa's, and Mama asked me if a samurai was a sandwich. Now she talked about history like she'd read every book on the subject.

"Did you know that a whole mess of everyday people tried to march to Jerusalem from Europe to take the Holy Land back from the Muslims? Not that the land wasn't holy to those Arab folks, too." Mama laughed.

I shook my head, both amazed at all Mama knew and embarrassed at the stuff I was ignorant of. The talk of history pushed thoughts of my library so far back into my mind, I forgot about it for a time.

"But it's true. A whole army of people marched down there. Never made it, though. Those folks did it years before all the fancy knights and such plodded off to kill people in the name of the Lord. Heathens."

Mama told me how people packed up their whole families to go rescue the Christians of Jerusalem, but they all died on the way of starvation, disease, and enemy attacks. The Mama I knew as a child never talked about history or geography, math stumped her, and school struck her as a waste of her time. Now she could be a schoolteacher as far as I could tell, going on about the world that used to be like she was telling a story about her cousin who got stuck in a collapsed coal mine and spent a week there trying to pick his way out. She made it fascinating and real like I could just pack my bag and join those folks on the road to Jerusalem if I had a mind to. I enjoyed this new side of Mama and, although it made me feel like a traitor to my own heart, I actually thought Mama had the right idea in moving to Chicago.

We spent the afternoon in the library, taking turns reading to each other out of books. When it was my turn to read, Mama made sketches of buildings, roads, and clothes from that People's Crusade of nine hundred years ago. While Mama read, I just listened. Her voice would shift with the events, growing slow and deep when they were trudging down the road, picking up speed, and turning desperate if they were attacked, then rumbling and dripping if a storm caught them. Closing my eyes, I could imagine us sitting in her window seat, Papa in a chair beside us. Funny thing, Lara was there, too, standing next to Papa, her hand on his shoulder. I guess she belonged there now.

That evening, Mama took me to a place called a pizzeria.

They make a thing called pizza there by stretching out bread dough until it's flat like a cracker, kneading it into a circle, then throwing it into the air like a lasso. I laughed at the sight, knowing pizza was a food Mama would love to make almost as much as throwing a dish against the wall to enjoy the sound. Spinning that dough in the air looked like a lot of fun.

Then they added tomato sauce, cheese, and little eye-patch-sized pieces of meat Mama called pepperoni. She said the Italians brought recipes for pizza over from their home country and we played around with it here in the United States until we had the cheesy, hot, spicy pie Mama and I ate. I found out it's a good idea to eat pizza with a stack of napkins because it's messy. Seeing Mama grab up a piece of that pie and eat it with her bare hands, I knew where Mama got the idea of eating Lara's blueberry pie without so much as a fork.

After having a slice or two, Mama got to working out her set ideas, laying out napkins and menus like the backdrops of a play. I loved seeing Mama build the world we'd read about even if the buildings were made out of paper. And the construction only started there.

Wrapping up the remaining pieces of pizza, we brought them over to Mr. Carroll and made sure he'd settled in nicely before setting to work in Mama's apartment. I helped Mama build sets and draw out the patterns for the costumes. Using chalk to trace around the pattern we made for what Mama called a jerkin, a little coat thing men used to wear, I saw my hands cutting out the clothes Mama and I used to make for our homemade paper dolls. Back then, we used the laundry Mama took in from other people to fashion costumes for plays we thought up. Now, we were making costumes and building sets for real plays. I knew then that Mama had found a way to do what her heart had been leading her to since I was a small child. And that made me feel full inside. So full, I turned to Mama and said, "I'm glad you moved here."

By the spark in her eye, I knew Mama had a wry comment to throw back at me, but she said, "Thank you," and went right back to painting the rise in a road that disappeared over a half-painted horizon.

The hours passed as the scraps of fabric piled up on the floor and Mama's skin disappeared under paint. I kept myself busy cutting and pinning patterns, then I moved on to priming canvases with white paint. I didn't get far into my new job before the fumes started making me dizzy.

Mama had her eye on me, though, and when I shook my head to clear it, she jumped up saying, "That's the sign you're too tired to paint, girl. Go on to bed."

"Aren't you coming?"

Mama looked at her painting, then back at me, saying, "All right." She stood up. Pulling a drop cloth off a hook by the front door, she led the way to my bedroom.

"What's that for?" I asked.

"Us." Mama threw it out over the bed. "I'm too tired for a shower and we're not getting paint on my quilt."

The drop cloth crinkled like paper under us, but it didn't matter. We were too tired to be bothered by noise. In no time at all, I fell asleep, Mama's arm draped over me like it belonged there.

Love and Keeping Busy

I woke up with the image of Lara's old parlor filled with small wooden tables, people sitting at each one, reading books. Mama had gotten up before me, so I ran to find her. The bathroom door stood open a crack, steam pouring out like the room was a tea kettle. I went right in, shouting, "Mama, I think we should turn Lara's old house into a library!"

"And a fine good morning to you!" Mama shouted through the pouring water and the weird curtain between us that looked as glossy as the coffee shop countertops.

"Don't you think that's a fine idea?" I asked, touching the curtain. It wasn't cloth. The darn thing was made out of something slippery so the water just beaded right off. Fancy that.

"It's a wonderful idea, Nissa. That's a whole lot better than that big place just sitting there. But I'm not sure how many folks in Harper would find the time to read a lot of books."

"They should."

Mama peeked out of the shower, her face all wet, her hair soapy. "Should they now? Let's make a deal, Sweetie. We won't let the people of Harper tell us how to live and in return we'll keep out of their lives."

"Fine," I said, leaving the room. "I just think it's a good idea."

"And it is."

While Mama finished her shower, I wrote Papa a letter to tell him all about my library idea. I also told him about Mama's job and all the great things we made together. Still writing when Mama came out, I told her what I'd said to Papa, so she added a few little drawings of the set we worked on.

Mama made an envelope out of an old drawing, then glued it shut, saying, "Off to the shower now, before that paint becomes your natural color."

As soon as I pulled the slick curtain back, I realized I didn't know how to make the shower work. I knew how to fill the tub, but had no idea how to make the water shoot up the pipe leading to the shower thingamajig.

"What now?"

"How's the water get up there?" I asked.

Mama laughed. "There's a really big fella in the basement who blows it up there."

"Mama!" I gave her a shove as she came in to give me a hand.

"Well, you push enough water through that tiny pipe and it'll come out." Mama turned a knob between the hot and the cold faucets. "There, now the shower will work."

"Thanks."

Just like Papa said, hot rain makes your muscles loosen right up. I didn't try his clothes-washing idea though. I didn't think of it until after I'd already gotten in naked. I told myself I'd try it the next time I took a shower. All in all, showers are a grand idea. You get in, you get wet, soap up, rinse off, get out. Quicker than frying an egg. But, a good soak in the tub sets your mind and body to rest in a way a shower can't. The thing's too noisy and quick.

While I took a shower, Mama packed us a picnic lunch. We took it to a park. Now, I'd seen the parks President Roosevelt had people building on the side of the highways, but this place was a whole other animal. Instead of picnic tables and cut grass, this park had paths made out of cement, benches, a pond cut free of all the weeds, and flower beds everywhere. Mama and I wandered around, naming flowers, pulling weeds and drooping blossoms.

"We'll have to keep our eyes out for just what we want in the garden I'm planning for the roof," Mama said, snipping a daisy head to put in her hair.

"That'll be grand."

I took Mama's hand and we went over to the pond to skip some rocks. A few boys stopped by to learn the tricks of the trade. Mama showed them how to do a triple hop while I worked on my double.

Back home, Mama and I chased butterflies after a picnic, but in Chicago, we ate our lunch on our bellies and told stories about the folks who walked by. We imagined that the lady we saw with the bus token stuck in the fake fruit on her hat was Miss Bertha Kennedy who had come in from Elgin for the day to buy a new hat; little did she know Mr. Ellston Reynolds would be in a hurry and trip while she walked up the stairs to catch a bus, sending his token in the air and onto her hat. Miss Kennedy kept right on walking, didn't even hear Mr. Reynolds when he called after her.

Story making was as fun as ever. I missed the thrill of the chase, but butterfly hunts were Harper things—like wading in Sutton's Creek or counting stars on the roof. Chicago had its own thrills—like eating pizza, reading in libraries, making props, and visiting parks.

"Our backyards like a park," I told Mama as we headed home.

"It certainly is." Mama smiled, saying, "That's where parks started. People over in Europe had these big old gardens in their backyards with carefully planted shrubs in the form of mazes."

"Like the Queen's garden in *Through the Looking Glass*." That book gave me nightmares.

"That's right. Anyway, some folks decided to make a few of them open to the public. And there you had a park."

Walking by a man who had just started to grow a mustache, I thought of Papa and how he sure would love to hear about all the new things Mama had learned. I wondered if moving out of Harper would've kept our family together, so I said, "Mama, why didn't you just ask Papa to move?"

"What?"

"Why didn't we just move to Chicago as a family?"

"Now look who's trying to fry a chicken for the second time.

Stopping, I said, "Don't tease, Mama. I'm serious."

"So am I. Once you've made a choice—mistake or otherwise—you can't go back and try again."

"Would you if you could?"

"You live in wishes and you'll forget you're alive, Nissa. Let it be."

Wishing and worrying are cousins and it seemed like I spent half my life doing one or the other. Mama had a point. My life would be a whole lot different if I didn't prattle away my time inside my head.

"So be it."

"Good." Mama gave my hand a squeeze.

Mama had to work that evening, but I got to watch. Stepping inside the theater, I knew just why they called it the Sunburst Theater Company. A blazing sun nearly swallowed up the whole ceiling, casting out rays of orange, yellow, and gold in every direction. The pale blue walls sported billowy clouds while the night blue carpet held a pattern of white stars. Spaced out along the walls sat wooden boxes painted as dark blue as the floor with constellations on each side. The room made me dream of walking on air.

Mama said I could watch from above. Hanging in the basket they hoisted up and down to fix the lights, I had the view of a lookout in the crow's nest of a pirate ship. Everyone else worked hard to put the sets up for their fairy drama—a children's play, written by one of the cast members, called *The Masquerade*. It told the story of a fairy named Tetum and her best friend Alta. They pretended to be human so Tetum could court a man named Caspian, while Caspian and his best friend Lorenzo masqueraded as fairies to court the women. The set had as many twists and turns as the plot, so watching it go up was like seeing them build a maze.

I watched Mr. Keller walk around the room with a group of men who filled each constellation box with sand. I had no idea why they'd need boxes of sand. For a bit, I thought the audience was supposed to throw it at the stage like pixie dust, then Mr. Keller asked Mr. Larson, a stage hand, to bring the fire curtain down.

Mr. Larsen said, "I haven't got it rerigged yet, Mr. Keller. I'll have it done by tomorrow night."

"No, you won't!" Mr. Keller shouted back. "This place will not be placed next to the Iroquois in the history books. Do you hear me, Mr. Larsen?"

"Yes, sir." Mr. Larsen shuffled off to the rigging along the wall and climbed up a metal ladder to work on what had to be the fire curtain—a gray cloth as long and thick as the velvet curtain in front of it, but nowhere near as pretty. Still confused, I didn't get any of it straight until Mama explained it to me on the way back to the apartment.

"Mr. Keller's afraid of a fire in the theater," Mama told me in the elevator. "His mama and older sister were burned up in a theater called the Iroquois back when he was still a baby. The fire curtain didn't work and the place didn't have fire boxes. As a result, he's near about insane when it comes to keeping the fire boxes filled with sand and the fire curtain in working order, and I can't say as I blame him."

The thought of burning up made my skin itch. The idea of losing a mama like that made me wonder where Mama'd been while she was away. I had a whole drawer of Mama's letters, but none of them ever mentioned where she'd been before she decided on settling in Chicago. My curiosity started to fill my head with questions, so I asked Mama, "Why didn't you ever tell me where you went when you left Harper?"

Stepping into the apartment, Mama didn't say a word. Pouring herself a glass of water, Mama drank half of it down before she said, "I didn't want you thinking I was off having fun while you were heart-heavy over wondering where I'd gone off to."

"Were you?" The thought of it made me feel sad.

"I won't say I never smiled. But I sure wasn't happy. That's why I came back to say good-bye."

"So what did you do?"

Sighing, Mama said, "I'll tell you all about it, but let's get into bed first. My legs are about to give out under me."

She handed me a glass to get my own water, then headed for her bedroom. I joined her there after I'd had a drink and slipped into my own pajamas. As we nestled into bed, Mama said, "I'm too tired to tell all tonight, Nissa, so I'll make you a deal."

"I'm listening."

"Each day you're here, I'll give you one stop on my winding road to Chicago."

"I'll sign on that dotted line."

"Good," Mama gave me a squeeze. "Now, off to bed."

With a kiss on the forehead from Mama, I headed to my room, thinking that with Mama having been gone for a smidgen over a year, she'd have enough stories to keep me in Chicago until Christmas. My mind didn't settle on just how that made me feel right off, but I sure did enjoy the immediate benefits of our little arrangement. When I woke up the next morning, I expected Mama to tell me a story that day, but the truth came out in bits and pieces. I spent my time putting all the pieces together.

After a breakfast of cold cereal on the fire escape, we went straight to the roof. Funny thing, when we came out on the roof of the building, we walked through a door in a tiny little hut of a thing that reminded me of an outhouse. The roof itself was a flat, tar-papered surface kind of like a man-made cliff. You could walk up to the edge and stare down at the city—the cars on the street zipping around like ants on a honeyed countertop.

Mama's garden space looked more like a theater stage at first. Using wood browned with age, Mama had built up a platform long and wide enough to be mistaken for a small barge. A knee-high edge went around the outside to keep all the dirt on the platform and give the roots room to grow.

"Why's it so far off the ground?"

"I've got trays down there to catch the water," Mama said, taking the steps up to the garden. "Come see."

I joined her. We looked at all the deep, black dirt and had a fit of toe envy. Both of us shucked off our shoes, tossed them onto the roof, sunk our feet in deep, giving our toes a wiggle.

Mama gave a sigh of happiness. "Nothing like dirt between the toes."

"Except mud."

"That's right." Mama laughed.

"How'd you get all this dirt?"

"You know that park we went to?"

I nodded.

"They built it through one of those work programs from the government—tore up the whole block, took down buildings to expand the park that was already there, dug up flower beds and sidewalk space. They had plenty of old wood and dirt left over. After they shut down for the night, I borrowed their wheelbarrow and went to work."

"You stole it?"

"Stealing's when you take something and keep it. Do you see a wheelbarrow?"

"No."

"All right then." Mama headed down the steps. "Let's go find Mr. Carroll to—" Mama turned around right quick, saying, "*borrow* his truck, so we can go buy some flowers."

Laughing, I said, "Sounds good to me."

Mama led the way to Mr. Carroll's apartment on the third floor. A note hung on his door saying he had a job to do in apartment 7E, so we headed up there. The door stood open. We walked in calling, "Mr. Carroll?"

"In here," he answered from the kitchen. We found him fixing a cupboard door. "They were in such a hurry to put these up, they hung the doors crooked."

"Mr. Keller bought this place in an auction and only had a few months to switch the whole place from a hotel into an apartment building so he could start collecting rent before he ran out of money to pay the mortgage."

"It shows." Mr. Carroll tested the door. "The place looks thrown together." He pointed to the doorway where they hadn't bothered to plaster over the edges after they cut the hole in the wall to put the door in.

"More work for you." Mama smiled.

Mr. Carroll nodded, the hint of a smile curling his lips. "The less I think of home."

"Mind if we borrow your truck?"

"Not at all." Mr. Carroll gave Mama his keys.

"Have a good day," Mama said, walking back to the front door.

Mr. Carroll leaned out of the kitchen as we got into the hall. "Miss Heirah?"

"Yes."

"I just wanted to thank you again for the job."

Mama looked around. "Might be enough work here that you could convince Mr. Keller to hire a few other men to do this job or that. Piecework for a flat fee."

I could see by the "get my meaning" look in Mama's eye that she had this planned out ahead of time.

Mr. Carroll's smile said he knew, too. "Sounds like a good idea."

We met an old woman pushing a shopping cart as we headed toward the elevator. "Are you coming from my apartment, Heirah dear?"

"Yes, Mrs. Bateman. Mr. Carroll's fixing it up nice. You be sure to tell Mr. Keller what a good job he did for you, now."

"I have already." Mrs. Bateman patted Mama's arm. "He came and rehung my bedroom door yesterday."

"He's a find." Mama laughed. "You have a good day, now."

"You, too." The old woman walked off and I couldn't help thinking that the building Mama lived in wasn't much different than a town. Folks stopping each other in the halls like most people do on the street, talking and sharing news. There was a theater, something Harper didn't even have. And a coffee shop. All they needed was a general store. Mama seemed to fit right in. Maybe people in the building kept their opinions to themselves.

"Who did all the handiwork before Mr. Carroll came?" I asked as we got into the elevator.

"Me," Mama answered. "You think I like living like a pig with no shade? I've been so busy for the last six months, I could hardly find the time to breathe, let alone clean."

That cleared up a lot for me. I now knew Mama didn't write because she'd been tending to thirteen floors of apartments plus doing her work for the theater. That made me feel a whole lot better about Mama not keeping her promise.

And my mood improved even more when Mama took me to a place called the Evergreen Nursery. We had to drive near to an hour to get there, but it was worth the trip. They raised plants there of every shade and variety, from green chives to red trees. There was a whole building devoted to flowers, blossoms from door to door, and that building was long enough to shelter a herd of cattle from a tornado, not that its green glass walls could offer any kind of protection.

Mama and I wandered for the longest time, smelling and naming and planning. Once we started deciding on what we wanted, Mama called over one of the workers to start loading up our pallets of flowers—we picked snapdragons of crimson, peach, red, white, and yellow; daisies in purple and white and pink; funny little flowers called Jewel Boxes that looked like bright colored caterpillars lying lengthwise over stems; a whole family of seeds from herbs to carrots; gardenias, begonias, marigolds, morning glories, ivy, zinnias, and finally roses. Mama and I saved those for last.

"You know, I should have brought a bare root with me."

"Papa could send you one." Seemed odd what with being in the city where Papa bought the bare roots for the roses and Mama wanting one from back home, but I understood. Those were her roses. They belonged with her.

"No, I want to bring them up. I'll do it on the next trip."

My heart got a healthy dose of excitement when Mama said that. She made it sound like coming down to Harper would be a regular thing.

"So, we need to decide what color roses we'll plant."

"Won't they freeze up here?"

"Not if we pack them in hay for the winter."

I nodded. In the end, we settled on tea roses in all the shades they had. The back of the truck was plumb full. We even had to bring some of the flowers into the cab. Seeing all of the flowers we'd picked out, I wondered how Mama was going to pay for it all.

"We have enough for all this?"

"We?" Mama rubbed my head. "Are you making money I don't know about?"

Mama meant it as a joke, but I didn't feel like laughing.

"You forget, Nissa, I've been working three jobs for the past six months—set designer, costume designer, and handyman. I'm a wealthy woman." Mama tapped my nose. "Besides, you see that grove of pine trees out there, sprouting up with plans on being Christmas trees in a few years?"

She pointed behind the flower building to a field of pine trees. I nodded.

"That's what I did with my Saturdays." Mama wiggled her eyebrows. "Mr. Carroll wasn't telling me anything I didn't know when he said keeping busy doesn't give you time to think of home."

Mama walked off to settle up our bill and I stood there thinking my mama missed me enough to plant a field of Christmas trees.

Enough

"I branded cattle in Texas," Mama told me as we sat at a table in The Silver Spoon folding programs for the play that night.

"Branded cattle?"

Mama laughed. "Well, just one."

"How'd you end up doing that?"

"I took a job as a cook on a ranch. I brought coffee out to the men while they branded. They let me brand one steer to show me how it's done."

"What was that like?"

"Evil. I did it so I could say I had, but seems awful cruel to burn an animal. But I suppose that's better than seeing a man shot for taking the wrong cow."

"People get shot for stealing a cow?"

"It's been known to happen."

I imagined Mama in the full cowboy getup-blue jeans, leather gloves, a hat—putting her knee down on a cow's side as men held the animal to the ground. Mama'd make a good cowboy, I decided.

She had the strength, the spunk, and the love of the outdoors. Mama's only problem was that she didn't know how to ride a horse.

As we folded programs, Glenda kept coming by and picking some up to pass out to customers. A few folks shook their heads and refused to even take the program. Others looked interested, but left it on their table after they finished their meal. I began to wonder if anyone would show up. What with so many people out of work, I figured folks didn't have the money to spare for going to the theater.

That night, Mama and I dressed up in our Sunday best, then sold tickets at what used to be the check-in desk. The line for getting in went clean around the block. Mamas brought their kids in by the hand, dragging and fussing. Grandmas brought their grandchildren. And even a few papas came. All of them looked like they'd come for Sunday services.

I had grasshoppers hopping around in my chest and the closer it got to curtain, the wilder they got. I finally decided I'd better take a walk if I wanted to keep from exploding. A trip around the block seemed like the right idea at the time. I had to weave through the crowd to get out, but I figured I'd have a clear path once I got around the corner. Wrong again: I met up with another line. In this one, there were no mamas in fancy coats dragging kids in frilly dresses or tidy suits with shiny shoes. These folks looked like they'd been living in the clothes they wore for some time. In fact, I could have met any one of them on a street back home during harvest. I felt silly for wearing my new yellow church-going dress. And guilty for eating the greasy old hamburger and fries I'd had for supper, knowing those folks were probably hungry.

Turning back, I wondered what they were all waiting for. I asked Mama when I went inside. Handing over the tickets she held to Darla, Mama stepped aside to tell me, "Those folks are waiting to see if there are any seats left."

"Left?"

Mama nodded to the crowd in the lobby, saying, "After these folks have all paid for tickets and gone in to sit down. Mr. Keller even waits for the houselights to go down for the pre-show."

"Why?"

"Mr. Keller doesn't want those ritzy folks to know the others are coming in. You see, these folks are paying as much as five dollars a ticket. The folks out back only pay a nickel."

"Really?"

"That's what they can afford."

It didn't seem right for the folks out back to have to use another entrance and sneak in when the lights went off, so no one could see them. It was then that I realized I hadn't seen but one or two faces like Miss Rinnie Lee or Mrs. Villeneuve in the crowds coming through the front door. I'd seen plenty of dark faces in the line out back. So much for people up North being color blind.

By the time I sat down for the play, I was sour enough to sweat lemon juice. That mood didn't have a chance to last. I'd never seen a play and truth be told it's like seeing a magic trick unfold. The stage lights went on and in my mind I knew the people up there were only acting in costumes my mama made, dancing around sets my mama built, but part of me believed those folks were fairies and fancy folk accustomed to dancing at balls and courting people with pixie dust and flowers. When the curtain came down, it hit me like a slap in the face. There was no half believing in fairies any longer.

"Mama," I leaned into her. "This is magic."

"I'll say." The distance in her voice made me look closer. Seeing the skin on her arm, I realized she had more bumps than a back road. Watching a play gave Mama goose bumps!

I near about cried I was so happy for her. Still, a part of me ached. Why couldn't Harper, Louisiana, have a theater? Or if we'd just moved to Chicago, Papa would be sitting beside me, clapping like all the folks around us—not just for the play, but for Mama, her costumes, her set, and her happiness. Instead, it was just me and Mama. And like Mama said, that had to be enough.

Telling Tales
and Picking Names

The next morning, Mama came in with a garden hose. I followed her into the bathroom to see her unscrewing the tip of the tub faucet so she could screw the hose on. She even had a little thingamajig to make the two threads match up. Standing, she said, "Feed the hose out the window while I go out on the fire escape to catch it."

I did as she told me. Mama leaned way out and I did my best to wiggle the hose over to her. After two laugh-filled failed attempts, Mama shouted, "Just throw it, Nissa!"

Swinging the hose like a lasso, I let it fly. With a shout of surprise, Mama caught ahold of it. "Now that's a throw."

Mama ran up the fire escape, saying, "Turn it on when I give you the okay."

A minute or so later Mama gave a *whoo-hee* from the roof and I turned the water on full blast. As the water chugged up to the roof, I wrote a letter to Papa telling him about the great play Mama helped put on and how much I wished he'd been there to watch it with me. My thoughts didn't cooperate enough to come out as written words when I tried to tell him about Mama being a new person in Chicago, so I just crossed out what I wrote on that subject and signed my name.

"Shut her down!" Mama shouted.

I laughed thinking how it must look to the folks down below seeing a hose going out a top floor window to the roof. Too bad they couldn't see the garden it fed. If I had my way, every window in Chicago would have a box of flowers hanging down and those stark buildings pointing up into the sky could have ivy growing off of the roof. I wondered if an ivy vine could grow from the top of the *Chicago Tribune* building to the ground. That'd be a sight—Chicago's own brand of kudzu.

"We're going to have to ask Jacob Carroll to put in a pipe up to the roof," Mama said, coming into the bathroom to help me draw in the hose. With the hose curled up in the tub like a snake, we headed for the stairs.

Planting our snapdragons in a spiral of color, Mama told me how she helped repair a roof after a sandstorm in Oklahoma. She'd been waitressing in a cafe in some small town called Garven when the storm hit. Mr. Henfield, the old man who owned the place, couldn't afford to hire a man to fix the roof, so he tried to repair it himself. Even raising a hammer made him cough and wheeze. Mama said to heaven with all that and grabbed a hammer, then Tarzaned her way up to help out.

"Mr. Henfield near about fell off the building when he saw me." Mama laughed. "He screamed, 'Miss Russell, you'll fall.'"

"What'd you say?"

"Only if I scare as easy as you, Mr. Henfield."

I laughed.

Mama shrugged. "Of course, I wasn't up there for more than an hour before Mr. Henfield started bartering with free meals to bring a man in there to finish the job."

Cattle branding, roof repairing, waitressing, and tree planting was only the beginning of Mama's long list of occupations. She said she only stayed in each place for a short time—long enough to get paid so she had money for the next leg of her trip.

Each day that passed, I joined Mama on another adventure as we tended our garden, worked on the costumes and sets for the next play, helped Mr. Carroll build the permanent prop room behind the stage, and snooped around Chicago.

On Monday, Mama and I cleaned hotel rooms in northern Oklahoma while we planted an herb garden. Putting up walls in the prop room on Tuesday, we travelled to a factory in St. Louis that makes cloth. Mama said the machines made so much noise you could still hear them in your head while you slept.

"Took a month to get that sound out of my head," she said. "And on top of that the place was so humid my lungs were starting to sweat."

By Friday we'd moved on to picking rock in the fields of southern Illinois. With all that mental traveling and interesting work, I hardly ever thought of home. I forgot all about the two-week trial period I'd set in the beginning. The weeks just rolled by as we made our way through state after state, job after job, until it was late-July and time to move all of Mama's things down to the prop room and start staking our bean plants. I opted for the staking job.

I'd just finished a nice old web of string when Mama burst out of the roof door, shouting, "Nissa! Your papa's coming!"

"You're telling a lie," I said, standing.

"Not if my tongue were on fire. He says he can't wait to see you any longer, so he's coming up on the train next Tuesday."

I could have done back flips all the way to Louisiana. Papa was coming to Chicago. He'd see all the fine work we'd done. And if he stayed long enough, he'd have a chance to see one of

Mama's plays. "Hot jam!" I did a little dance and Mama joined me. We stomped on a few beans, but it didn't matter. Papa was coming to Chicago.

Mama's adventure tales made it bearable to wait for Papa. Each day, I heard a new story of how she worked her way around Chicago until she met Mr. Keller in a grocery store buying oranges. Mama typed letters for a lawyer, worked the switchboard in a hotel large enough to put up the entire town of Harper for the night, and checked coats in a fancy restaurant that had a man playing a piano in the dining room.

By the time Papa's train pulled into the station, I felt like I'd travelled half the country. Seeing Papa step off the train, I ran full out to give him the longest hug possible. Squeezing him tight I noticed Papa's smell. I'd always been so hooked on the scent Mama carried with her no matter where she went that I never quite learned Papa's. Seeing him again showed me I'd known it all along. Papa smelled of ink laced with dust.

Saying our "missed yous," we let go.

Then Mama asked, "Where's Lara?"

Papa smiled, but it looked like he had to try real hard to keep it there. A fake one I could spot a mile off. "She's coming tomorrow."

"Really?" I asked, not believing him.

Mama got a spooked look in her eye like Papa'd told her there was a hailstorm coming and she had to protect her garden.

Patting my shoulder, Papa said, "That's right. I wanted some time to spend with my girl."

Mama's voice went flat as she said, "To prepare her."

"Heirah." Papa glared at Mama.

"Tell her, Ivar. She's going to find out sooner or later." Mama walked off, disappearing in the crowd on the platform.

I wanted to follow her, but I had to know Papa's secret. "What is it, Papa?"

150

"Let's go somewhere we can talk."

Papa tried to lead me inside, but I stood my ground, saying, "Tell me, Papa."

"You're going to be a sister again." Papa's smile was real this time. The kind that made the skin under his eyes curl up into smiles of their own.

Back in Harper, I thought being a sister would be a mighty fine thing. Standing on the platform, knowing Mama had walked off on account of the fact Lara was having the new baby with Papa that she never could, made it all seem awful.

"You're upset." Papa squeezed my hand. "Come on." Papa led me inside. Sad, I just went with him. Seeing a bench, Papa drew me to it.

We sat down facing each other. "Nissa, tell me what you're thinking."

Thinking the place smelled of coat, sweat, and spoiled food, I felt crowded, hot, and angry. Why could Lara have a baby when Mama wanted one so bad? I hated Lara all over again. How many things would she take from Mama?

"I wish you'd never met Lara Ross."

"Do you, now?" Papa sighed. "You'd wish that baby right back to where it came from?"

I'd done it again. Gone and wished when I had no right to. "No."

"You don't want to be a sister?"

"It's not that."

"Your mama?"

I nodded.

Papa folded his hands in his lap. "I can't speak for your Mama, now when she's close enough to do it for herself, but you have to know Lara's been wanting to have a baby for some time now. Long before she ever met me."

"Is that why she married you? So she could have babies?"

Mama told me that on the cattle ranch they paid folks to bring a stallion into the stall with a mare, so they could make a foal. The whole thing sounded ungodly to me. And so did marrying a man to have a baby.

"Nissa." Papa turned away. Looking at me a moment later, Papa said, "Sometimes your thinking can be so wicked. Lara and I got married to be a family. That means a lot more than just having babies."

What did that make Papa, Lara, and me? Where would this new baby fit in? Right between Lara and Papa, I suppose.

Without looking at him, I asked Papa, "Just how do you figure Lara, you, and I make a family?"

"I'm not going to answer that, Nissa." Papa's voice had gone stiff with anger. "As I see it, you stand to gain the most by answering that yourself."

Standing, Papa said, "Now, show me the way to your Mama's."

"Don't you have a suitcase?" I asked, glad I could put my mind on something simple.

"I'll go get it and meet you at the front door."

When we reached the apartment, Papa stepped in, dropped his suitcase, then walked right over to a wall full of practice paintings. "So these are the little murals you told me about. They're mighty fine. A miniature view into someplace like those Viewfinders they make." Papa held up an imaginary Viewfinder to make his point.

"Never thought of it that way," I said, staring at a view of a cathedral from the new play.

Mama came out of her bedroom saying, "So what do you think of the place?"

"Nice furniture." Papa nodded.

Smiling, Mama shook her head. "Same old Ivar."

"Nissa tells me you've reinvented yourself."

Hearing Papa talk about what I'd said in my last letter made me feel like a spy. I thought I'd crossed all that out. Did he treat it like a secret message and decipher it?

"Really?" Mama looked at me, but I couldn't read the thoughts in her eyes. "Well, I'm doing what I can."

"If the freight wouldn't send us into the soup lines, I'd say we could ship up some of the furniture from our place. Lara's got enough furniture in her old house to fill up two homes."

"That's mighty nice of you, Ivar, but I'll make do."

"We can build new furniture," I told Papa, feeling like I should defend Mama against handouts.

"Can we now?" Mama came up and put her hands on my shoulders.

"We've done it before," I said, thinking of Aunt Sarah's wedding box, and of course, Mama made me the best dressers under the stars.

"Then we'll do it again." Mama gave me a squeeze.

I looked at Papa. He seemed happy enough to burst a belly button with the smile on his face.

"So," Mama leaned a little to the left, pulling me with her, then swung over to the right, saying, "I suppose we'll have to think up a name now. Sound like good dinner conversation to the two of you?"

I said, "Sounds dandy." But really, I was just glad Mama felt happy enough to dream up names for the new baby.

"You could read me the phone book," Papa said. "I'm starved."

"All right then," Mama said, leading the way to the cafe.

Papa ordered enough food for two.

"Isn't Lara the one eating for an extra person?" I asked as the waitress left.

"Funny," Papa said, making buck teeth.

"How about Harold?" Mama asked. "Wasn't he a king of France?"

"I bet you're thinking of Henry," Papa said.

"Wasn't he a king of England?"

Mama and Papa talking about kings? I'd be more surprised by hearing Peter Roubidoux singing "Mary Had a Little Lamb."

"That's right!" Mama slapped the table. "Harold was the English fella who was killed by the Normans. Poor man, he became king, then died nine months later, barely enough time to even bring a baby into the world to be his heir." Mama sighed. I knew then that part of her heart ached for the babies she'd lost. I held her hand under the table. She smiled at me.

"Well, all that time in the library's paying off." Papa laughed. "Speaking of libraries, you should have heard Lara's response to your idea, Nissa."

"What'd she say?"

"She went to pacing the house, whispering to herself, 'My house a library? A *library*? Couldn't quite tell if she hated the idea or was just trying to get used to it. She kind of had the same response to finding out she was pregnant. Started telling anyone within speaking distance like she didn't believe it and wanted everybody to know so they could convince her."

"I know that feeling," Mama said with a smile, her eyes looking like she saw all the way back to the time she found out she was going to bring me into the world.

"What was it like when you found out I was going to be born?" I asked.

"I'll answer that." Papa hopped in his seat like a schoolboy, excited to have the right answer for a change. "She went to eating watermelon at every meal, taking her baths in the pond out back, and sewed her way to May. Nissa, you had enough clothes to wear a different outfit every day for a month."

Mama laughed. "Remember that little one with the daisies I sewed all over it?"

"Yes," Papa nodded. "She looked like a little old pot of flowers.

"And then she turned it purple by sitting in a bucket of blueberries when we went picking up on Crotter's Hill."

Mama and Papa had travelled back to a place I could never go—a time when they were a young married couple living near the Amite River. They loved each other then. A love that makes you want to bring someone else into the world to share it with. That's the love of a family—the very thing Papa had tried to tell me about in the station. Now Papa loved Lara enough to need someone else to share it with. Someone other than me.

Tours and Tantrums

Papa asked for a tour of the place. Starting on the first floor we made our way to the theater. Papa took a real liking to the prop room. He stood in front of Mama's paintings and stared like he half expected someone to come walking out of them if he waited long enough. After a time, he turned to leave, saying, "Now you never have to worry about running out of wall space for your murals, do you Heirah?"

"No, sir," Mama said, heading into the theater.

Coming out onto the stage, Papa froze. Laughing, he said, "I don't even like the idea of standing up here."

Mama said to me, "On our wedding day, your Papa told me it was a good thing we didn't have guests or he never would've been able to say the vows."

"Papa?"

"Put more than three people in the room and I feel like turning into a clam." Papa curved his back to suggest shriveling up.

"So you let Mama do the talking."

"Like I'd ever give him room to say a thing."

Papa raised his eyebrows at that idea, saying, "You all did a wonderful job fixing this place up into a theater."

"Well, the dressing rooms still look like a row of closets, but it's coming along good."

"Let's take Papa up to the roof!" I shouted.

Papa didn't say a word as we came out onto the roof. Walking around the edge of our garden, running his hands through the morning glories and ivy growing down the sides, he went clean to the other side before he turned around to say, "Heirah, I think you could make a garden grow in the desert."

"Here's to hoping I never live to test that theory." Plucking a morning glory, Mama raised it like a glass.

"All right." Papa leaned over to pluck his own. "Here's to a great success for your next play!"

Taking a blossom, I lifted it in the air, but no toast came to mind. What did I want? Mama had her theater and the best roof-top garden ever planted. Papa had a new wife and a baby on the way. Me, I was living with my mama again like I wanted. Only trouble was I needed my papa, too, and not just on visits. Finally, I said, "To happiness."

"In whatever shape it comes," Mama added and we tapped our flowers together. Drinking down our pretend champagne, we threw the petal glasses over our shoulders and laughed.

When the laughter died away, Papa said, "Lara's visiting her sister in St. Louis. I better call down there and tell Lara I'm here safe."

Locking arms with Papa, Mama started to drag him toward the stairs, saying, "You don't fool me, Ivar Bergen. You're calling to see if your new mama is taking good care of herself."

"You caught me." Papa smiled at her. When Mama smiled back, I think she really meant it.

With Papa down in Mr. Keller's office, I finally had a chance to talk to Mama. "Do you feel bad about Lara having a baby?"

Mama dropped down onto the garden steps. "Part of me's happy enough to float. The rest of me feels like dead wood."

"I wish I could join you on the happy part," I said, sitting down.

"You aren't happy?"

I shook my head.

"Don't want to share your Papa with the new baby?"

I shrugged.

"Hmm." Mama sighed. "I guess I'm just nervous."

"About the baby?" Here I'd been thinking Mama would be jealous that Lara could have the baby she always wanted when Mama was worrying Lara might lose the baby. I started to wonder if I really knew that much about Mama and her feelings.

Rubbing her arms, Mama said, "The baby will be fine."

"So you're not worried about the baby?"

"I am, but it's a silly fear. Lara's young and healthy. Nothing will go wrong." Mama drifted off, her eyes taking on a far-off look.

"I'm sure you're right, Mama," I said, patting her knee. For the first time, I thought Lara might lose the baby. Maybe that fear had been nagging at the back of my mind from the beginning. Seeing things that way made me wonder if I didn't feel guilty for living when all those babies died—Benjamin and the two Mama never even got to hold. Why did I get to stay in this world when they didn't? That didn't seem right at all.

"No more thinking!" Mama shouted, jumping to her feet. "We need to be doing."

"Doing what?"

"I say we sew the little tyke a quilt."

"With suns all over it to remind the baby of the Sunburst Theater!"

"All right." Mama headed for the stairs.

We were already digging through the fabric box for sunlike remnants when Papa came in. "So this is where you two got off to."

"We're making the baby a quilt," I told Papa.

"Are you now." Papa stood over the fabric box. "Can a bumble fingers like me join in?"

"Now there's a fine idea." Mama slapped the floor. "Take a seat and start hunting up some sun."

"Sun?" Papa asked, sitting down.

"The quilt'll have suns all over it."

Papa nodded, then dove right in. The three of us cut, pinned, planned, and sewed into the night. A row of suns hung on the wall by the next morning when Papa got up to get Lara at the station. Mama had gone to take her turn running the elevator. She took the early shift so she'd have time to paint before Lara came.

"Want me to go with you?" I asked, coming out of Mama's bedroom where I'd spent the night, so Papa could have my bed.

"Only if you want to go."

I didn't really. Train stations stink. And I'd never even started to miss Lara, but I could tell by the pleading look in his eyes that Papa wanted me to go, so I said, "Wouldn't miss it."

Rubbing my back, Papa said, "Thank you, Nissa."

Standing clear of the crowd on the platform, we waited for Lara's train to come in. Shouting to be heard above the racket, Papa said, "You ready to warm bottles, change diapers, and entertain a baby?"

"I've got to do all that?" Truth was I had fun doing those things for Benjamin, but I didn't have to tell Papa that.

"Well, I thought you'd like to have a hand in taking care of the baby."

"Sounds like a lot of work."

"And fun." Papa leaned into me. "Remember playing peekaboo with Ben in the study?"

Bennie'd sat on an old blanket in the middle of the room. Papa and I'd squatted below the windows, a stack of books between us. I'd grab a book, hide my face behind it, then Papa would say, all excited, "Bennie, where's Nissa?" I'd pop out. Bennie'd shake with laughter like a pinata on a string. Papa took his turn with me asking Bennie, "Where's Papa?" Bennie bounced with laughter.

I felt a bit of laughter chasing around in my chest as I remembered those times. "That was fun."

"There she is!" Papa sprang forward as Lara hobbled down the steps. I stood there shocked that a person's belly can really stretch that much in two months. Papa ran up to her and swung her right off the bottom step. Lara squealed like a little girl.

"Oh, Ivar." Lara swatted Papa as he put her down. There she went getting scared about nothing again.

"Lara," I said, nodding to her as I came up.

"Don't I even get a hug?" Lara asked, holding her arms out to me.

When Mama was pregnant with Bennie, I used to hug her belly, then her. "Have to give one to Baby," we used to say. I couldn't bring myself to do that with Lara, but I did give her a squeeze.

"How are you?" she asked as I backed away.

"Fine," I mumbled.

"What?" Lara yelled over the noise of all the people coming and going. "I can't hear you."

"I'm fine!" I shouted.

"Just fine?"

"I'll go get the luggage," Papa said, disappearing.

He had a habit of doing that when things got tense between Lara and me. We all knew he did it to give the two of us time to talk. That didn't make me any happier.

The last thing I wanted to do was talk about me, so I

pointed to Lara's belly, asking real loud, "So what's it like to be pregnant?

Lara leaned close so I could hear her real clear. "You ever had someone sit on your stomach?"

Mary Carroll sat on my tummy for stealing her brand-new harmonica once. It proved a mighty effective way of getting it back. She was so heavy I threw it at her to get her off. "Yes, I have."

"Well it's like that only you feel like you're carrying the person around inside your stomach instead of on it."

The thought of it made my insides ache, so I changed the subject. "When's the baby supposed to be born?"

"Sometime after Halloween."

In that flash of an answer, I realized that Lara had been pregnant when Mama came to town. "Why didn't you tell me before I left Harper?"

"Things got mighty complicated around that time. We didn't want you to have any more serious things to think about."

There go those fool adults again, planning my life without my knowing it. Deciding what I should and shouldn't know. And here I'd been teasing Mary Carroll for not knowing April was pregnant when my own stepmother had a baby inside her. Turns out, I was more clueless than that baby on what was going on in the world around me.

Papa showed up with the suitcase and a bottle of orange coke. "Here you go, Lara. You must be thirsty."

"Indeed." Lara took the orange coke. "But you know this means we better head ourselves toward a bathroom. Another thing about being pregnant, Nissa, is that your bladder shrinks up to the size of a teacup."

Lara took a long drink on her coke. I could taste the tongue-tingly orange in my own mouth. "You get a coke for me, Papa?"

"Yes, ma'am." Pulling a bottle from his coat pocket, he handed it to me. As he picked up the suitcase to leave, I saw that he had two more bottles of coke in his other pocket. One for him and one for Mama. Just the way it should be.

Mama met us in the lobby, paint spattered and sweaty. She eyed the coke in Papa's pocket, had it out and down her throat before Lara even had time to finish saying hello.

"How do, Mama-to-be?" Mama's smile came with a grape coke mustache. I had to laugh.

"Great, thank you," Lara said as she and Mama looked at me to see what tickled my funny bone.

I wiped my mouth to show Mama she should do the same. Mama raised her eyebrows at me, but then turned back to Lara saying, "You all right? Are your feet ready to burst?"

"I feel like I'm walking in skin-tight galoshes filled with water."

Sure enough, her ankles looked all puffy. Having a baby certainly was a body-altering experience. I'd never really thought on it much before. Maybe it was on account of me being older this time. Or perhaps knowing that my body could carry a baby now changed my thinking. No matter what it was, the whole thought of being pregnant scared me to shivers.

Going upstairs, we found out Mama and Mr. Carroll had made quick work out of turning the parlor-prop room into a proper parlor. Using planks, they'd made a park bench-style couch, then covered it with blankets and pillows. The table in front of it was nothing more than two milk crates, but they worked just fine for Lara, who had all the news in the world for Mr. Carroll. He tried to slip out when we came in, but Lara pulled him back in saying, "Don't go, Jacob, Patricia has deemed me messenger."

We all sat down, some of us on kitchen chairs, to hear how April'd grown round, Teddy'd got himself a job working in the

Journiette fields, Simon had started helping the Minkies out twice a week for a dime, and Mary Carroll had her eyes on Gary Journiette, but Mrs. Carroll kept her close at hand by making her do the housework for April. Hearing Lara talking about Harper made me long for home. I also felt guilty for not writing to Mary after all this time.

Mr. Carroll sat in his chair asking all sorts of questions. What did the doctor say about April? How was Winston's job at the feed store? Was young Anthony keeping out of trouble? The answers delivered, he sat back for a moment, then said, "My how I wish I could be there when my first grandbaby comes into the world."

"You should be," Papa said. Lara loudly agreed.

"I'd lose my job," Mr. Carroll said.

Mama spoke up, saying, "I got you the job, I can make sure you keep it."

"You certain about that, Miss Heirah?"

"If I don't, your salary comes out of mine."

"I couldn't do that."

"Then you'll just have to trust me." Mama patted him on the back.

"I don't know."

"I can offer you a two-way train ticket as a congratulations present," Papa told Mr. Carroll.

Lara's eyes flashed with anger, but she didn't so much as part her lips.

"Oh, I sure would appreciate it. I send whatever money I have down to Pat and the kids."

"Of course." Papa nodded. "I'll send the money when it's close to her time."

Mr. Carroll stood up shaking his head, saying, "I don't know how I can ever repay your kindness."

"You'll know when the time comes," Mama said, getting up to open the door for him.

"Good night all." Mr. Carroll waved good-bye. We sent him off with our best wishes. That is except for Lara. She looked mad enough to spit venom.

"Ivar," she said as the door closed. "Can I talk with you in private?"

"Is this about the ticket?" Papa asked.

"In private."

"If it is," Mama broke in. "I can chip in."

"I just want to speak to my husband in private," Lara told Mama.

Papa started to speak, but Lara jumped in, yelling, "Can't we just once have a conversation without everyone listening in?" She didn't even give Papa a chance to answer, before she added, "This isn't her family anymore!"

Mama leaned close to Lara's ear, then whispered, "Words spoken in anger start fires you can never put out, so I'd hold my tongue if I were you."

"No." Lara stood up. "I won't. Ivar is my husband. We have a right to our privacy."

"Indeed." Mama nodded. "You go right into Nissa's room over there and have yourselves a private talk. But something tells me you don't have the power to hold your voice down. Heck, half the floor already knows you're mad. You don't have the benefit of a yard between you and your neighbors here, Lara."

Lara stormed into my bedroom with Papa half a step behind her all the way.

Mama turned to me, her eyes wide, saying, "And I thought I had a temper!"

I didn't want to move. Why'd everything have to fall apart when the lot of us got together?

164

"Don't worry, now." Mama shook my knee. "Your papa and I had fights that you could hear clear to the Gator when we first got married. Granted, I didn't have a first wife hovering around me, but things will iron themselves out."

"Mama, you got divorced."

Mama laughed. "True enough. But that happened when we stopped fighting, not because of it. And if I know your Papa, he won't make the same mistakes twice."

Love Thyself

Swallowing the urge to sneak into the bathroom and listen in on the fight raging in my bedroom, I followed Mama up to the garden. We'd already weeded, so we just picked flowers, then sat on the wall along the edge of the building and released petals into the wind. It takes a special flick of the wrist, like skipping rocks, to get them to fly. Sometimes they flew right back into our faces, sticking to our cheeks like rainwater. But mostly they sailed out into the air, swaying down toward the ground.

Watching them float made it look easy until an eddy of wind came along and smacked them against the side of the building. Then I didn't think so much of floating anymore.

After a bit, I said to Mama, "You wishing it was you who was having a baby?"

"Heavens, no." Mama twirled a flower stem. "I'm having enough trouble raising the child I've got."

"I'm trouble?"

Mama grabbed my face and shook it. "Stop your worrying."

I tried to smile, but she'd scared me.

"No, you're not trouble. I've made all the worries I've got. Built them special." Mama dropped the stem. It didn't float at all, just plummeted toward the ground. "I used to think I'd be happy with a large family. Being surrounded with children seemed like the happiest way to live. Then I realized it wasn't the people I longed for, but the way they felt about each other."

"How so?"

Mama held out her arms. "When you hold your newborn children in your arms, they've got a power over you so strong you fear your soul might collapse."

Her words gave me a twitter in my chest.

"They're so clean and new. Not a sin on them. And it was that clean love that made me think my love for other people would make me feel whole, fill up the emptiness I've got inside me, but it can't. You've got to love yourself first. Make yourself whole before you can really love another person. See, I didn't know how to love me, so all my love for other people got twisted and spoiled."

"Like your love for Papa."

"That's right. I resented him for being happy. Your papa's got a rare gift—that calm he's got at the center of his soul. Do you know what I mean?"

I sure did. That deep, private part of Papa that allowed him to stay calm in almost any kind of storm; so that meant he loved himself. Sounded selfish, but God says do unto others as you would have them do unto you. So you can't love someone if you don't love yourself. I nodded.

Mama continued, "Folks always told me the way I did things was wrong. At school teachers said little girls raised their hands before they spoke and they didn't talk back. The pastor at church felt sure I'd burn in hell for thinking God wasn't a man or a woman, just God. The folks in Harper are no different. They think, Heirah

Rae with her fancy name and funny ways believes she's too good for us." Mama put her knees to her chest and held on tight. "I thought, how could so many people be wrong about me?"

The answer was as clear as the tears on Mama's cheeks. All those folks couldn't see double. They spent their whole life looking at things the same way. If they'd stop a minute and try to hear the thunder in the crash of a plate they'd know Mama wasn't the crazy one. She had it right.

"But they are, Mama." Speaking brought tears to my eyes, too. "All of them."

Mama smiled, the tears spilling over her lips. "Thank you, Nissa." Gripping my hand, she said, "But I had to find that out for myself. Go someplace and figure out just who I was." Mama laughed, then shouted, "And fall in love with myself!"

I laughed with her.

She leaned forward so our foreheads almost touched, saying, "So hear me well, Nissa girl, don't go looking to other people to be happy. You fill your ownself up." Mama tapped my chest.

I nodded, but I had no idea how to go about doing such a thing. Mama'd gone off on a whirlwind of adventures. How could I do that? Mama found a way to have all the things she wanted; a place to paint, to build, to grow, and a way to be with me. Truth was I didn't even know what I wanted besides sharing my life with Mama and Papa.

I heard the creak of the door and expected to see Papa, but Lara came around the corner instead. "Nissa." She said my name, but her eyes were on Mama. "Can I have a minute with your mother?"

"Sure enough." I slipped off the wall, then headed for the stairs. The pull to stay and eavesdrop was so great, I held the railing all the way down to the landing, praying that Mama and Lara would make their peace.

Papa sat down on the quick-made couch as I came in. I told him, "Mama's up there talking to Lara."

He nodded. Seeing my face, he put his hand to my cheek. "You been crying?"

"A little."

"Sit here," Papa patted the couch. "Everything's going to be all right, Nissa."

"Why's Lara still so mad at Mama? Doesn't she know you don't love her in a husband-and-wife kind of way anymore?"

Papa pulled at the seam of his britches, then said, "You remember what Lara said about your mama when we went on that picnic by the Amite."

Oh. That picnic. I'd lost my head and tried to swim across the river, and it near about cost me my life. I tried not to think about that day, but I did recall Lara saying something about how much she respected Mama, but she'd always been afraid to talk to her. I'd never even thought of anybody being afraid of Mama before that. Well, sure there was Chessie Roubidoux with her silly ideas about Mama brewing voodoo, but that woman didn't have two good senses to put together.

I whispered, "She said she wished she had the courage to talk to Mama."

"That's right. Lara always admired your Mama, envied her even. Now that she's living in your mama's house, married to your mama's husband, and having a hand in raising her child, she sees your mama as a threat. All that respect has turned to fear and jealousy."

"How ugly."

Papa didn't so much as twitch his head. "Lara knows she's let her fear take over. Now all she has to do is find a way to overcome it."

"So she's going to talk it over with Mama?"

"She's trying to right now."

Papa and I sat there and stared at the door like two people in the waiting room at a hospital wondering if the doctor's going to come through with good news or bad. Mama had a way of either tearing people down or building people up. I prayed she'd find a way to tear down Lara's fear and build up a friendship.

The laughter came first—Mama sounding like a banging screen door in the distance with Lara chippering away like a bird. Papa and I looked at each other and smiled. Talk about getting more than you prayed for—Mama and Lara came through the door out of breath and two shades darker than the red snapdragons Lara had sprinkled in her hair. Covered in petals, leaves, and dirt, the two of them looked like they'd uprooted the whole garden.

"What happened?" Papa and I asked together.

Staggering, Lara caught her breath, then said, "Heirah and I expressed our feelings in a manner befitting two ladies." They burst out laughing like two old men leaving a saloon.

"You had a flower fight!" I shouted.

"That's right." Mama said, tossing a stem at me. "And it felt darn good."

I wished I'd been there, but it sure felt nice to know they'd gotten all their feelings out in the open. God willing there'd be no more explosions.

At dinner in The Silver Spoon, Lara even apologized to me for losing her temper. Then, by way of explanation, she asked me, "You know how they say when you're pregnant, you eat for two?"

I nodded.

She said, "Well, I think you feel for two as well. My emotions are strong enough to make the devil say amen."

"Don't go thinking that ends when the baby comes," Mama said, waving a hamburger bun at Lara as she poured ketchup with her other hand.

"Oh, don't tell me that." Lara shoved three fries into her mouth. We didn't have a restaurant that served such food in Harper, so we all ate like it was our first meal in a month.

"Don't worry, you'll be too tired to care." Mama laughed.

"Tell me about it," Papa said, throwing a few fries onto his burger.

"Why?" Lara asked. "Did you get tired of hearing the baby cry and watching Heirah get up?"

"Watching?" Papa and Mama both burst out laughing. "Not a chance," Papa said. "I got up when Heirah got up. She used to say . . ." he turned to Mama as if he was the director of a play.

And they both said, "We made this baby together, we're raising it together."

All the grown-ups thought that was mighty funny, but I couldn't help thinking that Mama and Papa hadn't stuck to that plan. So I didn't find it funny at all.

"Well, Heirah, which room do you think we should make into a nursery?"

"Truth is when I got pregnant the third time, not too long after we moved into Harper, I thought of moving Nissa up to the front room across from mine, so the baby could be in the back of the house where it stays cool. It's also quieter back there."

My room may be quieter and cooler, but it also had my last year's birthday present from Mama. We couldn't move a ceiling along with my furniture, so I didn't like the idea at all. "What about my night sky? "

"I'll paint you another one."

"Then there'd be two!"

Papa said, "Why not move our bedroom up to the front and put the baby in the room across from Nissa's?"

"Now there's a compromise." Lara shook a fry at Papa.

"I like that much better," I said, taking a sip of my malt.

We spent the whole evening planning for the baby—where to put the crib, what kind to get, who to have on hand when the time came, and names. Harold got thrown out in favor of Stewart or Michael and they thought a girl named Hillary or Emily would be nice. I thought all of the names sounded like people you'd meet at one of those schools where everybody wore uniforms and went to plays wearing white gloves and shiny shoes or a suit with brass buttons. How awful. My vote was for Cole or Rayanne, but I kept my mouth shut since they all seemed to be having such a good time talking to each other.

That night, as Mama and I tried to go to sleep, Mama said, "It'll be so nice to have a baby in the house." She made it sound like she'd be there.

"I suppose so."

"You still don't sound so happy."

"Do you think Papa and Lara will raise this baby together?"

Mama took my hand and squeezed it tight. "Your papa and I are still raising you together, Nissa. We just don't live in the same house."

"Well, I hope they do that for this baby."

"There's no way of knowing," Mama whispered. She fell silent for a moment, then she said, "I'll be sorry for leaving you until the day I die. But I had to do it."

I never said anything back to Mama. I still didn't believe leaving was the only answer. Maybe Harper hadn't given her any other choice that she could see, but there had to be one. Still, finding it now wouldn't do either of us any good, so I gave Mama a kiss on the cheek, then rolled over and went to sleep.

Building

The next morning, I walked into the parlor to find Mama sitting on a stool painting a panel from a backdrop. Seeing me, she said, "There's no natural light down there in that dungeon of a prop room. At least here, I can get the light from all the rooms." Mama pointed at the light streaming in from the kitchen, bedroom, and bathroom with her paint brush, sending little specks of black paint all over.

"Why not build yourself a painting place up on the roof?" The idea came to me as quick as a wing beat.

"Now that," Mama shouted, "is a grand idea I'd thank heaven for!"

Kissing me madly about the face, Mama added, "So I guess I'll just have to thank heaven for you." Bumping noses, we laughed. Mama said, "And I'm not waiting. That studio gets started today."

Mama headed right out the door, leaving me standing there like I'd just been splashed by a passing car in a rainstorm.

"Nissa?" Lara said as she shuffled her way to the kitchen a moment later. "You all right?"

"Yes, I just lit a fire under Mama. And that's always a shocking experience."

"I'll say." Lara shook her head as she put the coffeepot on the stove. "I thought you had an arm for throwing things, but your mother's a whirlwind."

"You two had quite a flower fight?"

"Indeed. That woman has enough energy for twelve people."

"Always has."

"I am sorry I lost my temper."

"Everyone seems to have an itchy trigger finger when it comes to feelings these days."

"I'll say."

"You happy about being a mama?"

Lara got all shaky with excitement. "I get the chills just thinking about it."

"Papa's real good with babies."

Lara touched my face. She'd never done such a thing before. At first, I wanted to pull away, but her fingers felt so warm and kind, I couldn't do it. "He's a wonderful father." Dropping her hand down onto mine, she gave it a squeeze.

Complimenting me and Papa in one fell swoop, it felt so nice I could have kissed her, but I didn't. I just said, "Isn't he though," and smiled real big.

Papa came in, looking like an old man, his face full of creases from sleeping on a wrinkled sheet. Standing behind Lara, he put his arms around her belly, then kissed her at the bottom of her neck, resting his head on her shoulder. "Morning."

"Morning," Lara hummed back.

I felt like I was watching a picture show I shouldn't, so I stepped out of the room.

A bit later, Papa called out, saying, "Where's your mama?"

"Off to build herself a studio on the roof."

"Really?" Papa came out of the kitchen buttering a slice of bread.

"Don't you want to toast that first?"

"Your mother doesn't have a toaster and my stomach's not willing to wait on stove-toasted bread." He took a bite.

"Mama said the prop room didn't have enough natural light for painting, so I said she should build a room up on the roof."

"Now that's a fine idea. You seem to be full of them lately."

"Does that mean you like my library idea?" I asked, figuring that was what Papa had in mind.

"Sure thing." Papa licked the butter off his lips. "I'd be your first and most frequent customer and not just because I'm your Papa."

"Thanks, Papa."

"But, do we have to build it in my house?" Lara asked, coming out of the kitchen with a cup of coffee for her and one for Papa. "I mean, we might sell it."

Papa said, "It's one way to keep the house in the family."

I told her, "Besides, that place might not sell for some time now." When I'd written the idea down, I'd thought it was a mighty fine one, but it seemed too out of reach now, even though we were talking seriously about it. I'd lost the thrill that goes along with thinking up a great idea. I needed to borrow some of Mama's energy, I guess.

"I suppose so." She blew on her coffee. "But it seems so funny to have a library there, people walking in and out like they own it."

Papa said, "It's not much different than having a new family move in."

"True enough, but I wouldn't be visiting my own house as a customer in that case."

"No, you'd be a visitor." Papa squeezed her knee.

Lara pressed her face up to the side of Papa's, saying, "Point made, Mr. Bergen."

I looked away as they started whispering to each other. Getting up, I said, "I'm going to find Mama to see what she's up to."

Papa called, "Wait, Nissa."

"Yes?"

"Lara and I?" He motioned to Lara who was in his lap by this time. "We also came to see if you wanted to come home."

Papa's question gave my emotions a stir. I missed Papa, but Mama and I had never had so much fun. I had to go home sometime, but why now?

"I don't know, Papa."

"Well, you think about it." Papa looked scared or maybe just sad. Lara didn't seem to mind.

"Uh-huh," I nodded.

"All right then."

I left before the thought of missing Papa made me agree to go home with him. Staying with Papa for the day wasn't even an option anyway. Lara was off to visit her grandmother's sister in Joliet and Papa had newspaper business to attend to. Mr. Hess had only agreed on letting Papa travel to Chicago if he brought back a report on the job market in the big city. Folks down home were itching for a way to bring in some money. And Mr. Carroll's success had everyone looking North.

I searched on almost every floor for Mama before I found her in the storeroom behind the theater. Lumber laid all around her, Mama was sprawled out on the cement floor, drawing with chalk. "I think the roof'll hold a room about the size of the parlor if I build it far enough a way from the garden."

"It'll be grand, Mama."

"Indeed," Mama said, pecking the floor to put in a few flowers outside the studio. "Mr. Keller said I could build anything as long as his roof didn't leak."

Mama and I planned and prepared all afternoon. When it came time to start hauling lumber upstairs, we brought Mr. Carroll in to help. He went on about all the things he'd been doing—fixing showers, something he'd never even seen before coming North, radiators, radios, and even a tricycle for some little kid on the third floor.

"This is fine work," he said, as we started up in the elevator for yet another trip. "I could do this for a good, long time. They could keep that mine closed for all I care."

"Does that mean you'll move up here?"

"Maybe so." He nodded. "But I'd have to talk with Patricia."

Mary always said she missed living up North, but I sure didn't like the idea of her leaving Harper. Not unless I had the chance to stay in Chicago with her and Mama. But then I'd only be able to visit Papa. And there was winter to contend with. I couldn't imagine living life in a city like Buffalo where it got so cold the water on your eyeballs got stiff, and Mama said in her letters that Chicago got just that cold.

As we spread the tarp over the lumber to protect it from rain, I said, "Mama, Papa asked me to go back to Harper."

"You ready to go?"

Looking at the pile of wood, I couldn't help thinking Mama and I still had a lot of building to do of one kind and another. "Not yet."

Mama winked at me. "Glad to hear it."

As we walked to the stairs, Mama said, "But don't you forget that the longer you stay the more worried your papa's going to get. He wants you to come home."

"What do you want?" I asked, opening the door.

"Before I tell you, I want you to promise me something."

"What?"

"That you'll do what you want."

"I will."

Mama shook her head. "Since when? Girl, you've been like a second skin to me all your life. And I'd have to say I love it, but I know it isn't right."

"Being close is a good thing." It did my heart good to know Mama still thought of us as being two of a kind.

"Not that close. You've got to give yourself room and plenty of it. Learn from your mama's mistakes."

"I promise, Mama."

"Well then, I want you to stay with me until you're too old to chew your own food. But that's motherhood for you." Mama went pounding down the stairs in her leather boots.

And I felt light enough to float.

God's Plan

Papa didn't want to leave without having some alone time with me, so when he finished his research, he left Lara to watch Mama build, then took me to the zoo.

Going to the zoo made me think of all the animals Mama and Papa'd brought alive through books. Mama used to read to me about things such as stuffed animals who came alive, like Winnie-the-Pooh and the Velveteen Rabbit. Mama read the books like a play—acting out each voice with a new twist on her own. Me, Papa, and whoever happened to stop in for the performance, be it Mary Carroll or Ira Simmons, sat and listened to Mama like some folks crowd around a radio—all leaning forward and skin tingling with excitement.

Papa read in a mighty different way. I'd wander into his study and find him wedged into his reading chair. When I was small enough, I'd just climb right in there with him. Tangled together, we'd dive into a book, Papa reading, me resting my ear on his chest, so the words echoed in my head. With Papa, I'd ventured into Kipling's jungles, rode the waves with Long John Silver, and even solved a case or two with Sherlock Holmes. The study always made me think of distant places—a world in pages. And Papa loved giving me tours of those places. We'd read many a book together filled with wild animals like elephants and chimpanzees, but no printed page can make a person understand what it's like to stare at an animal big enough to clean your gutters with its trunk and heavy enough to turn the rest of the house into rubble. Then there are those wild monkeys acting like little human children with their running and teasing. Of course, little kids are more apt to eat mud pies than bugs off the skin of a brother, but I could have watched those furry little devils for days.

But Papa wanted to talk, so we went to the bench in front of the bear pen and had us a sit down. "Tell me what you think of staying with your mama."

I didn't want to make staying with Mama seem so grand that Papa thought I liked it better than living with him, so I said, "It's just fine."

"How fine?"

"Why?" I asked, pulling a piece off the cotton candy Papa'd bought me. I still couldn't get over how much it tasted like honey-coated sand when I first put it in my mouth.

"Do you want to stay?" Papa made to smooth out his mustache but he'd shaved his face clean.

"Yes," I nodded. "Mama's going to be real busy. She'll need the help."

"For how long?" Papa didn't even look at me when he asked that question.

I figured he feared I'd never go back to Harper.

"Papa, I won't stay here forever. I'll be back in Harper before you know it."

"That's what you want?"

I always figured that's the way it had to be. I was born in

Harper, raised in Harper, I half expected to die there. But did I want to go back?

"I don't know."

Papa bowed his head, his hands shaking. "I want to be fair to your mama, but I can't see letting you live up here year-round."

"You'd miss me too much?" I asked, because Papa had to know Mama would feel the same way.

"That and other things," Papa said, getting up. He started to pace.

"Like what?"

"Schooling. If your mama had her way, you'd never go to school."

I recalled the time Mama tried to convince Papa I didn't need any more schooling than he could give me at home. Mama didn't like the idea of spending her days alone.

"They've got plenty of schools here in Chicago," I said, thinking that Mama had changed her mind about a lot of things; school could be one of them.

"In Chicago?" Papa turned to face me. "Where there are thirty children in one classroom? That's just for your grade, Nissa, and one teacher. There could be as many as three hundred in the seventh grade alone in any of these Chicago schools."

"Oh." That was almost a quarter the size of Harper. I didn't want to go to school in a small town.

"And you could get lost trying to walk home from the store or hit by a car. People drive like it's a speedway around here." Papa'd gotten so flustered he'd started to raise his voice.

"Papa." I stood up. "Mama said something to me yesterday that I really have to think about."

"What's that?"

"She made me promise to do what I wanted. Truth is, I don't know what I want. And until I do, I'm staying here."

"Fair enough." Papa ran his hand through his hair. "But you think long and hard about what it means to live in a city, Nissa."

"I will, Papa. I promise."

"Good." He kissed me on top of the head. "Now eat that silly stuff and let's go see what those gorillas are up to."

The gorillas perched on logs to catch the food thrown by two kids standing outside their cage. I watched with my eyes, but I couldn't keep my mind from running back and forth between Harper and Chicago. Back home, everything I knew waited for me: Mary Carroll, school, the house, Mama's garden—which I guess wasn't really hers anymore—Sutton's Creek, Grower's Meadow, and the Crocked Gator. Then there was Papa. Life wasn't quite full without him there.

Chicago had libraries, zoos, the theater, the roof garden, and more noise and hustle than the inner workings of a sawmill. And what of Mama? Life seemed to slow down without her.

"If I lived in Chicago, when would I see you?"

"I'd hope we could spend the holidays together. All of us," Papa said, leaning on the railing. "Your mama could bring you down for Christmas and stay until New Year's."

"Really?"

"I'd insist."

"And you'd visit Chicago?"

"As often as I could, but that's a pretty expensive trip, and a long one for a baby."

I'd forgotten about the baby. The chattering of monkeys in the background made me remember Bennie's crying tirades. He'd get it in his mind that he wasn't tired and cry until he ran out of air, his voice turning raspy and his tears mixing with gasps. I got to thinking he would die if someone didn't get him out of bed. Mama said he'd cry himself to sleep, which he did, but it seemed like we all had to pass through a corner of hell for him to get there. Having a baby in the house means an hour doesn't pass when you aren't reminded that you've got a new life to feed, bathe, and protect. I didn't realize how much that was true until Bennie died and the days seemed to stretch on forever, long and empty.

My emotions started tumbling. I went dizzy with feelings of sadness, guilt, confusion. Dropping down on a bench, I wondered if I wasn't learning just what it's like to go crazy.

"Nissa?" Papa came and sat next to me.

"You ever wish you could flip a switch and shut your mind off like it was a flashlight?"

"Don't I ever." Papa tried to smooth out the crease in his britches.

"But wishes are a waste of time and energy."

"You're awful young to be believing that."

"It's true, isn't it?"

Papa leaned his head back. Staring up at the sky, he said, "I don't know. I guess I always figured wishing about the things you can't change gives your mind a little hope where there is none. I'm not sure if that's good or bad."

"Bad." I threw the rest of my cotton candy in the trash. That stuff's sweet enough to rot a hole clean through your stomach. "You spend all your time wishing instead of getting on with your life."

"Like your Mama."

"What?"

Papa smiled. "Your Mama always wished she'd find a way to make her home in Harper. And when that wishing didn't work, she left."

"And sent me to wishing she'd come back."

"Now, here we are." Papa slapped his thigh.

"Stuck wishing we'd found a way to make it all work as a family."

"That'd be wishing away Lara and the baby, Nissa. I couldn't do that."

Grandma Dee used to say God's plans are like the thread in a quilt. If you're patient enough to wait for the quilt to be finished you can see the pattern the thread makes, but by that time you don't see the thread itself until you get real close. Was that God's plan from the beginning? Mama and Papa would stay married long enough for Mama to have the strength to fly out of Harper. Papa'd remarry and start a new family. And me? Now that thread I couldn't see right off. Trouble was, I didn't even know where to look.

Destination Unknown

I'd spent so much of my life trying to make sure Mama was happy or convincing myself Mama loved me no matter what, that I forgot about living life for my own sake. Now that I had a chance to do just that, I had no idea how to go about it. Sometimes in school, I'd sit staring at the same math problem knowing the answers where there somewhere hiding among the numbers that blurred before my eyes. The answer didn't come until I slipped the paper into my bag and started home. I'd be thinking about how the rocks under my feet could have been boulders back when dinosaurs roamed around, then it'd hit me. The math problem would fall together like a deck of cards when you shuffle them just right.

I suppose my mind had been trying so hard, it couldn't see the answer until I gave it a rest. I figured the problem at hand couldn't be much different. If I just went about my day like nothing hung over me, my mind would relax and sort everything out.

Working on Mama's studio seemed like the perfect distraction. Mama showed me how to drive a nail straight, build a sturdy frame, and work a power saw. Let me tell you, running one of those things is like grabbing ahold of a gator by the tail and forcing it to chew through wood. We hung doors, plastered walls, slipped in time to sew the new baby's sun quilt, fitted windows into sills, laid floors, and planed shelves. My hands got as rough as raw wood, my arms felt like they had rocks floating around in the biceps, and I started hammering nails in my sleep. All that work sure got my mind off my problem, so far off that I rarely thought about it. When it cropped up, I was usually slipping into sleep and too tired to pay it any mind.

Then the answer struck me like a nail through the backside, an unfortunate experience I'd lived through when I slipped on my way into the new studio and fell fantail first onto a discarded board.

The day I discovered my destination, Mama and I went on a shopping spree. The studio was a coat of outside paint away from being finished, so we had some celebrating and space filling to do. Shopping seemed like the perfect way to do both. Mama led the way to an antique store just a few blocks from the apartment. The owner had a closet full of books he'd found tucked away in furniture he'd bought through estate sales. For a penny a volume, Mama bought enough books to fill up all the shelves we put up. We paid more for the wagon we dragged the books home in than the books themselves.

Mama started putting the books up as soon as she dragged the wagon through the door. "Now I'll have my own private library."

Seeing those books go up on shelves I had a hand in building, hearing Mama say "my own private library," my thoughts shocked me more than the sudden pain of a nail stabbing into my flesh. I really could build a library in Harper. The studio I stood in was partly a product of my own hands. If I could build a studio on the roof of a building in Chicago, why couldn't I build a library out of a house in Harper? The library would be my own. Something I did for me. Not Mama. Not Papa. Just me. Sure folks from town would come to check out books, but they'd know I was the one who put them there.

Where would I get the books? Papa said he'd donate all of his. The Villeneuves had a whole wall full next to the piano Mrs. Villeneuve used to give folks lessons. I spent my one and only piano lesson staring at the shelves wondering what books they had that Papa didn't. That prompted Mrs. Villeneuve to tell Papa not to send me back until I could keep my mind on the keys. She thought I was too young, but I really just had my mind on other things. The Villeneuves always gave a stack of books to the church sale every year; they'd surely give me some for a library. Then there was Papa's friend in Baton Rouge who could send me books. I'd beat the bushes if I had to, just to find the books.

"Nissa?" Mama shouted.

"What?"

"Where'd you drift off to?"

"My library in Harper. I'm going to build it."

Mama looked stuck, like she didn't know what to do. "Really?"

"That's right. I could build it out of Lara's place, and go around door to door collecting books. You showed me every-thing I need to know. I can build the shelves, fix anything that breaks."

Mama stood up real slow like she was trying not to spook a nearby animal. "Sounds like a plan."

"I'm going to make it work, Mama."

"I bet you will." Opening the door, she said, "You better get packing."

"Do you like the idea, Mama?" I felt nailed down to the floor all of a sudden, like I couldn't move if I didn't know what Mama thought.

"It's your idea, Nissa. Not mine." She smiled, but it was a weak smile that could be hiding sadness. "You're the one who's going to make this happen."

Mama was letting me go. If I left then, the library would be all mine. I had to walk out that door and leave Mama behind. The thought chilled me like a towelful of ice on a swollen limb. The cold went straight to my heart. Mama knew what I had to do. She turned and started putting books on a shelf.

To break the hold Mama had over my life, I had to leave. I faced the door which stood open to the roof and Mama's beautiful garden. I told myself I had every right to leave. Like Mama, I had to walk out on someone I loved to build myself a future, something I could call my own.

Stepping outside, the air felt cool and smelled of coal. The rooftop seemed to stretch out like a sail in a strong wind. Reaching the stairs, I thought of a room just for children where they could build the stories they read in blocks or snuggle into a window seat with their folks to hear a book read aloud. The ideas tumbled into my head, sending me down the stairs all the faster, I could plant a garden in the back, flowers in the front, have a brunch on Sunday mornings after church, and folks could come to talk about books they'd read over the week.

I had my things packed before I knew I'd started—new baby quilt and all. Sitting on my bed, I wondered if Mama would make me buy my own ticket home. I only had a few pennies to my name. A few minutes later, Mama came into the apartment. Standing by the front door, she said, "Mr. Carroll's packing to join you."

"Is April having her baby?" Such timing could only be planned by God Himself.

"Soon enough. I asked him to go so you wouldn't be alone."
Mama spoke more to the floor than to me. "Besides, I'll need the
extra work when you aren't around."

I was about to apologize, but then Mama looked at me
and stared right down to my bare soul, a warning in her eyes.
Backing down now would hurt us both. "All right then."

"There's a train that leaves at 4:30." Mama opened the door.
"Mr. Carroll said he'd be ready."

The clock on the parlor wall said I only had a half hour before
I headed South. A long wait would be too hard. I pulled my suitcase off the bed, then joined Mama in the hallway. She grabbed
the suitcase and headed for the stairs.

Mr. Carroll met us in the lobby. He looked nervous enough
to be a new papa instead of a grandpa-to-be. "You're sure I won't
lose my job, Miss Heirah?"

"I'll explain everything to Mr. Keller."

"Shouldn't I go say good-bye?" I asked.

"Why? You'll be back," Mama said, pulling the suitcase up to
her hip before she walked out the front door.

Mr. Carroll carried my suitcase onto the train, leaving Mama
and I on the platform. Poking me in the belly, Mama said, "I
expect there to be a library in Harper when I come down for
Christmas."

"Papa said you can stay until New Year's."

"Then you'll have to build a room for me in that library so I
can keep out of Lara's way."

"I'll do that, Mama." I couldn't help smiling at the irony of
Mama sleeping in Lara's house while Lara slept in hers.

"Make me prouder than I already am, my girl." Mama gave me
a soul-touching hug. I started to cry.

"No tears!" Mama pinched my nose. "Tears are for wakes.
Funerals are for celebrating a soul's journey to heaven. And

good-byes are when you start saving up stories for when you see each other again." Kissing my cheek, Mama said, "Now get on that darn train before I kidnap you and lock you away."

"Yes, Mama." I kissed her, then ran up the stairs so the desire to stay couldn't catch up to me.

My heart shrunk a little as the train pulled away, but I knew I'd made the right choice. I could feel it like a warm blanket on a cold night—a tight, satisfied feeling deep down inside strong enough to carry me home.

Home Again

I fancied a surprise homecoming would be the best one possible. When we made our first stop, I begged Mr. Carroll not to wire home to Papa or Mrs. Carroll and hoped Mama kept just as quiet. As the train pulled into Harper, I found myself nearly hanging out the window to take in the country scent of rain-soaked grass with a strong trace of pollen thrown in. I could've stood on that platform and just breathed in the moist, scent-filled Louisiana air all day if it weren't for the fact that Mr. Carroll went straight home and I had to do the same if I wanted to be the one to break the news of my return.

Dropping my suitcase in the street in front of the porch, I hurried down the stretch of grass between our house and Old Man Beaurigard's. Water splattered under my feet as I tiptoed up the garden path.

I saw Papa walking down the hallway, reading a newspaper. Standing still, I wondered if he could feel me there watching him. Sure enough, he stopped, then looked out into the garden as if he expected to see a bird or a roaming coon. Instead, he saw me. Throwing the paper over his head, he came charging out, yelling, "Neesay!"

He whirled me into the air with a big old hug. Putting me down, he said, "You and your mama didn't have a fight, did you?"

"No." I shook my head, laughing at Papas excitement. "I came home with a mission."

"A mission?" Turning, Papa shouted into the house, "Lara, come see who's here!"

"I'm going to build the library, Papa."

"Good to hear it." Papa clapped his hands together. "This place could use one."

Lara came waddling out onto the back stoop looking far too much like one of the penguins at the Chicago Zoo. "Nissa! Welcome home."

Kissing me on the cheek, Papa whispered, "Give her a hug."

The only way I could get my arms around Lara was to stand on the step above her and lean down. "How do, Lara?"

"Fine." Lara smiled, her face looking as wide and happy as a two-year-old who just ate a juicy slice of watermelon. "I think the doctor was a little off with his due date. Either that or I'm carrying twins."

"Heavens, I hope not." I laughed. "Two babies in the house would mean we'd get no sleep for a year."

Rubbing her belly, Lara said, "It'd be worth it. I can't tell you how much I want to hold this little one.

"You'll get your chance real soon."

I stepped into the hall. It looked familiar enough, but I found myself running my hands over everything like the whole place might just up and disappear.

"Where's your suitcase?" Papa asked.

"Out front. I wanted to surprise you."

"You sure did," Papa said, heading through the house to get my suitcase.

As he went out the front door, Lara squeezed my arm, saying, "I'm so glad you're back, Nissa. This old house seems so large when you're the only person in it."

Did she actually want me around? And here I thought she'd cherish all that alone time with Papa. But I guess he still had to go to work. "It's good to be back."

"You must be exhausted." Lara looked around like she'd lost something. "We were planning a big welcome home party. But we didn't know you were coming."

"That's all right." I headed for the stairs. "A nap will do me just fine." I didn't know how to tell her, a coming home party couldn't do justice to my leaving home party.

"Well, your room's all clean. The windows are open and the curtains drawn so it should be cool in there."

"Thank you." Heading up the stairs, I called down over my shoulder, "Papa, I'm going upstairs for a nap before I fall asleep on my feet."

I really just wanted the time alone to soak in the old house. Boxes lined the hallway, so I figured Papa and Lara had made headway in creating a nursery out of Papa's old bedroom. I didn't want to think on any changes right about then, so I went to my room and shut the door. Staring up at the stars on the ceiling, I let my mind drift. The screen door on Minkie's Mercantile slammed shut, and Clem Thibodeaux called out, "Have a nice evening." Birds sang in the garden. Cicadas sent their charges through the air. I smelled pollen and cumin floating around with that line-dried laundry scent of crisp, clean sheets. Crawling into bed, I rolled around, laughing at the rumpling sound of fresh sheets. It felt so heart full good to be home.

"Nissa Marie Bergen!" Mary's shrill shout climbed the garden walls with her. In a flash she came lumbering into my window. "What makes you think you can come home without stopping by to see me?"

"I've only been home long enough to take a breath, Mary."

"Looks to me like you're fixing to take a nap."

"Well, I'm not." I slid out of bed to give Mary a hug. "It's great to see you."

With my hands on her back, I realized Mary'd cut her hair while I was away. The strands bunched up into curls around her neck. I'd never have guessed her hair got curly when she cut it short. It'd been at least shoulder length all the while I'd known her. "Your hair looks grand, Mary."

"Thanks." Mary blushed which told me she had a romantic motive for cutting it.

"Does Gary like it?"

Mary shrugged. "He doesn't so much as look my way.

"At least not when you've got your eyes on him."

Mary rolled her eyes. "Enough about Gray, tell me everything about Chicago." Going to my dresser, Mary pulled a tin out of the top drawer, saying, "I've been saving up for this day." Dumping a tinful of saltwater taffy, she plopped down on the bed. "Do tell."

I talked until my jaw was tried, half from talking, half from chewing taffy. My lips were no doubt as candy stained as Mary's. I could still taste the taffy sweetness even though the candy was long gone. Talking to Mary felt as natural as breathing, so telling her all about Chicago was like catching my breath after a long run.

I was just about to tell Mary all about my library plans when she flopped onto me, hugging my neck, and saying, "Oh, Nissa, I missed you something awful. Thought I'd have to start talking to Missy LaFavor if you didn't come home soon."

"You certainly were desperate."

We laughed. Then Papa knocked on the door, leaning in to say, "Folks are gathering on the porch to see you, Nissa. You better come down."

"All right, Papa." I headed for the porch with Mary a step behind me. Papa walked next to me, hugging me every couple of steps.

"It's so good to have you home," Papa said, letting go.

The whole crew was assembled on the porch: The Carrolls, Ira and Rinnie Lee, Mr. Hess, the Villeneuves, the Caveats, even Otis and Ira's brother Leo

"We want to hear about Chicago," Ira announced.

"And welcome you home," Rinnie Lee smiled at me, but she gave Ira an elbow in the ribs.

Feeling like a record with a too-deep groove, I told all my Chicago stories over again, everyone asking questions, shouting their guessed answers, and generally having a good time despite the sneers of the passersby who didn't take too kindly to black folks hanging out on the porch of white folks. But I would have wagered a pound of my own flesh that those same folks kept an open ear to all the talk on our porch so they could spread it around town.

A Matter of Choice

The ladies in the mercantile the next morning proved my bet to be a sound one. Mrs. Fisher and Mrs. Linzy hovered around the dry goods counter while Mrs. Minkie tallied up accounts. I'd gone in to do a little shopping for Lara, who felt a need to keep her feet up.

"A library?" Mrs. Fisher bubbled.

"Who would have thought of it?" Mrs. Linzy added like they were discussing a brothel.

"Here in Harper?" Mrs. Minkie shook her head. "Only Heirah Rae would come up with such a darn fool idea."

Dropping my basket onto the counter, I said, "The library's my idea. And a darn good one, too. If you ladies did more reading, you'd probably spend less time trash talking other folks."

"That's no way to speak to your elders, young lady," Mrs. Minkie snapped.

"I'll speak civil to my elders when they start acting like adults instead of gossipy children."

"I never." Mrs. Linzy covered her mouth in shock.

"And I suppose you'll be letting those filthy darkies into this library of yours?" Mrs. Fisher asked, the bubbles in her voice filling with steam.

"They're far cleaner than your mouth."

"That is enough. Out of this store this minute!" Mrs. Minkie came storming toward me, pointing at the door.

"Fine." Turning, I felt like I'd just fought a gator bare-handed and won.

"Nissa?" Lara called as I passed the parlor. "Did you get the sugar I asked for?"

"No, ma'am," I said, leaning on the doorjamb.

"Didn't I give you enough money?"

"Mrs. Minkie kicked me out of the store."

"What?" Lara leaned forward in disbelief.

"She threw me out for sassing her."

"What did you say?"

"They started trash talking my library idea, so I said they could do with a little improvement by reading a few books."

Lara gave a cry of surprise like she stepped on a loose board in a bridge. "You didn't?"

"I did."

Lara scrunched herself up in a ball of nervous energy. "Oooheee, what I wouldn't give to be standing right there when you gave old sourpuss Minkie a piece of your mind. Sit down here with me." Lara drummed the couch cushions with her feet.

I plopped down beside the tower of foot pillows.

"So, you're really going to make my house into a library?"

"Until it sells," I said, remembering her comments in Chicago.

"Oh." She gave me a nudge with her toe. "That place isn't going to sell. Not only will it be the first public library for miles around, it'll be the only one with a functioning bathroom."

"What?"

"The only one I've been to in Tucumsett Parish was over in Marshall and they had folks using old newspapers for toilet tissue in the outhouse out back."

"I thought we could even have Sunday brunches like they do at The Silver Spoon."

"You certainly won't be inviting the ladies from the mercantile for that." Lara laughed, slapping a pillow.

"They wouldn't come anyhow. They don't take too kindly to the idea of letting black folks check out books."

"I didn't think of that," Lara whispered.

"What's there to think about?" Mama always said if you started seeing people by the color of the skin your soul would go blind.

"Maybe we could set aside a room for colored readers."

"No ma'am!" I shouted, standing up. If Lara hadn't had a belly-ful of baby, I would've dumped her right off that couch.

"Now don't get excited, Nissa. I know they've got every right to read a book, but we want everyone to have a chance to use the library."

"The library's door will be open to all. If the narrow-minded folks in town can't see their way clear of black skin, then they can just stay away for all I care."

Lara looked at me like I'd just said I planned to walk around the edge of Mama's roof with my eyes closed. "That's a mighty brave thing to say. And you're right, but folks around town might not take to the idea."

"What are they going to do?"

"You don't want to know."

The tremble in Lara's voice made me think of the stutter in Mr. Beaurigard's. He stood head high to the kitchen stove when the Klan came to burn his family out. One of those sheeted ghouls threatened to cut Mr. Beaurigard's tongue out. That'd put a hitch in my voice for sure. Mr. Beaurigard knew what happened when black folks went where some people thought they didn't belong. The Beaurigards had built a house on Main Street. And I wanted to build a library that allowed anyone to walk right in the front door and check out a book. What a fool.

Mama always said folks in Harper preserved ideas like they did their garden crops. But they never replanted them in quite the same way. Folks around town held on to ideas that should have died on the battlefields of the war between the states like they came straight out of the Bible.

"What am I going to do?"

"I don't know, Nissa." Lara took my hand and gave it a shake. "We'll work this out. You, me, and your papa."

I nodded, but I didn't feel any better. What did we know of solving those kinds of problems? The person who would have a true idea of the things I faced was Mr. Beaurigard. "I'll be right back," I told Lara as I headed for the front door.

"Where are you going?"

"I'll be back."

I'd never been in Mr. Beaurigard's house. Not because I was afraid to go. He just never invited me. We always conducted our neighborly business in his backyard. As I stepped up onto his porch and my knees started to shimmy, I realized I really was afraid to go through his front door. Not quite sure what I feared, though. Did I think he'd set traps for white folks who had a notion of coming into his house? What a fool idea. Still, my hand shook when I knocked.

The shade went up on the window by the door. The room beyond was filled with shadows so I only saw a hint of his face, then the door creaked open a bit. "That you, Nissa Bergen?"

"Yes, sir."

"You needing s-something?" he asked, opening the door wide.

I nodded, but my words got all slippery and I couldn't catch ahold of one to get it out past my lips.

"What is it, ch-child?"

"I'm thinking of building a library," I sputtered.

"That's what I hear." He smiled, scratching his chin through his gray beard. "You need some b-books?"

"Yes, sir, but that's not why I came."

"Really now? So what b-brought you over here this morning?" He held up a hand. "Don't t-tell me yet. You come on in here and I'll make us up some lemonade."

As he let me in, he headed through the parlor to what I suspected was his kitchen. The parlor could have been a museum with its grand old photographs framed in wood as thick as a draft horse's collar, high-back velvet chairs, and tables full of little glass trinkets that would've had Lara foaming at the mouth with jealousy. The room looked too fragile to sit in, but Mr. Beaurigard came back with a tray of lemonade, saying, "S-sit down."

Perched on the edge of a couch, I tried to work up the courage to say what I came to say.

"Don't be n-nervous, child," he said, pouring a glass of lemonade. "We're old f-friends."

"Yes, sir."

"Sir?" He laughed. "This m-must be serious."

"I've been thinking about the library."

"Uh-huh." He handed me a glass.

My hands shook so bad the ice chattered like teeth. "I want all the folks of Harper to come and use it."

He nodded, keeping his eyes on my shaking hand.

I said, "All the people."

Sighing, he said, "Black and white."

"Yes, sir."

He shook like he was trying to chase off a chill. "You're p-playing with fire there, ch-child."

"I know."

"No you don't. A church built over in Vincentville when our boys came back from Europe was burned to the ground because it didn't have a colored balcony."

I had no idea the people in Tucumsett Parish did such an awful thing. I'd heard of church burnings and always thought the folks who lit the fire had come straight from the devil. Folks around town never spoke of it. I hoped they kept silent out of shame. I sure didn't want to watch my library burn to the ground, but the alternative didn't seem right.

"Lara said I should set aside a room for the black folks, but I don't like the idea. It's wrong."

"That it may be, but I'd rather have a room in a 1-library I can use than no library at all."

The thought of Lara's house burning with all those books inside made me feel singed. If I went along with the colored-room plan, I'd be no better than the folks who put up separate bathrooms and made colored folks eat in the back of a restaurant or sit in the last car of a train. I'd be dirty, cruel, and crooked.

"Don't let it pull you d-down, Miss Nissa. Most wh-white folks wouldn't even think to let black folks into a 1-library. They figure we can't read." He laughed. "Some folks may think you should keep all the d-doors in that library open, but they won't be the ones p-putting their lives on the line."

"Lives?"

"That's right, N-nissa. There's no t-telling when they'd put the torch to your library. Could be while you're in it."

"I never thought of that."

"Neither did the minister of that ch-church I was telling you about."

"He died?"

"Him and his f-family. They were living in the ch-church until their house was finished."

"Heavens." I couldn't imagine being trapped inside a burning building. The thought of it gave me the shakes all over again.

"G-give me that before you spill it." Laughing, he took my glass. Placing one of his wrinkled hands on my knee, he said, "I'm no B-booker T, but I know pushing for change too f-fast leads to bloodsh-shed. Now when you've lived enough of your l-life to risk losing it, you go r-right ahead and fight that fight. Not now, Miss Nissa. Y-you got a mama and a papa who'd be heartbroken."

"What would you do, Mr. Beaurigard?"

"Don't ask me, M-miss Nissa. I'm an old man who has lived a l-long time and seen enough of my own b-blood to know it d-don't scare me no more." Patting my knee, he stood up. "Y-you give yourself a little time. B-build up your s-strength for battles to come."

"Thank you, Mr. Beaurigard." I kissed him on the cheek which sent him to giggling.

As I got up to leave, he said, "You're we-welcome, now ch-child." He stood up and headed for the door. "You c-come back for books now, you hear?"

"Yes, sir."

"That's a g-good girl."

My heart had a war going on inside it. I loathed the idea of finding myself surrounded by flames, but I'd sure be a two-faced coward if I built a colored room in the library. I couldn't help thinking that now was the time to prove I had the courage to do what I believed in. But could I pay for that belief with my life?

I still had enough of the coward in me to know I didn't have the strength to risk that much and it made me feel like I'd started to shrink from the inside out.

Papa found me pouting in my room that afternoon. "Lara told me you found a stumbling block in your library plans," he said as he took a seat on the windowsill.

"Why didn't you ever tell me about that church where the minister and his family got burned to death?"

"Who told you about that?" Papa asked.

"Mr. Beaurigard."

"You talked to him about all this?"

I nodded.

Papa smiled. "Nissa, you can't solve all the world's problems. You've got to leave some of it up to the rest of the folks."

"I suppose, but having a colored room is wrong."

"You're just a regular old human being with a heart big enough to make the moon fall out of the sky."

"Papa." I shoved him. He leaned back toward me. We laughed.

"Lord, it's good to have you home."

I sat there a moment, feeling Papa's love for me, all happy and warm. Then I asked, "Do you think God would be mad at me for having a colored room?"

"I don't know." Papa got up. Kissing me on the top of the head, he said, "You'll have to ask Him."

After Papa left, I did just that. I prayed to God so I could know just what I should do. That left me with only one task—waiting on the Lord.

Waiting

The nice thing about waiting is you can do it in any fashion you care to imagine. Now God had a fine way of waiting for people to see the light, giving folks like April and Lara the miracle of childbirth, bringing silly lovers like Mary Carroll and Gary Journiette together, and dropping hints so folks can learn to fly proper before it comes time to fly home. I just hoped I'd see such hints when He sent them down. Knowing my patience couldn't compare to God's, but liking the idea of keeping busy, I decided to do my waiting by building bookshelves.

The first challenge to that plan was finding wood. Being a carpenter, I figured Ira would have a few good ideas on where I could scare up some lumber, so I went to his shop a few doors down from the Crocked Gator. A barn in another life, the shop smelled of sawdust and hay. Furniture filled the place, some of it in need of repair while other pieces were waiting to be finished. Mama had made my garden dresser there, so I kind of felt close to her as I walked to the back. Ira stood over a drawer as he planed it.

"Mr. Simmons."

"Miss Nissa." Smiling, he put the planer down on the drawer, then turned to face me, asking, "You taking up a poll?"

"Pardon?"

"A poll. You going around asking folks what they think you should do with your library?"

I don't know why I should've been surprised. Ira was no different than anyone else in Harper. He heard as much gossip as everyone else. But it still made me feel a little foolish somehow. There'd be no need for such a poll; all the gossip in town would come back to me in the end and I wouldn't have to do anything more than sit on my front porch and let the rumors drift in.

"No, sir. I'm looking for wood."

"For bookshelves, I reckon," Ira said, wiping his hands on the towel he kept in his back pocket—the same checkered kind of towels Rinnie Lee used at the Gator. "Well, you know I buy my lumber by the load, so I don't always get good furniture wood." Walking over to the far wall, he kicked a shin-high pile of lumber. "These here have ugly knots in them that I wouldn't want showing in a piece of my furniture. They'd make good bookshelves though. A few of them are warped, but the weight of the books'll straighten them out."

"What do you want for them?" I don't know why I even asked that. The only thing I had to trade were the clothes on my back and the furniture in my room and they weren't even mine in any real way. Papa paid for everything.

"A free pass into the colored reading room." Ira smiled like he'd be proud to go in the back door.

"You think I should have a colored room?"

"Now, I wouldn't say I'd want a colored room, but I'd have to admit that's what you should do. Unless you want to bring a whole mess of trouble onto yourself." Ira tousled my hair. "And I like you too much for that."

"Thanks, Mr. Simmons."

"Don't mention it." He laughed. "Heck, Leo tells me that most of the libraries he's seen won't even let our kind in the door—front or back."

"I'd pay you for the lumber if I had the money."

"Well, I don't have any books like Mr. Beaurigard or the Villeneuves, so just think of this as my donation."

"All right." I suddenly realized that the grapevine in town would do me some good after all. In no time, the whole town would know I needed books for the library and send them my way.

"I'll bring the lumber out to the Ross place this afternoon."

"Sounds mighty fine." I felt like I'd have to start putting rocks in my shoes to keep my feet on the ground. This whole library affair made me feel like dancing on a cloud.

Saying good-bye to Ira, I headed back home.

"There goes Miss Bookworm," Otis Dupree shouted from the back porch of the Gator cafe where he sat with Leo having some lunch.

"Do we get the root cellar or the outhouse for our books, Miss Bookworm?" Leo asked as I got closer.

"Haven't decided."

"Hear that, Otis?" Leo swatted Otis on the arm. "This nice little white girl hasn't decided just what she's going to give us reading black folks."

"All right then, Mr. Dupree, what would you have me do?"

"Build your darn library and leave us colored folks out of it. We can take care of ourselves."

"I sure don't want no little girl telling me what books I can read," Mr. Garver said from the next table.

I'd never thought of that. The blacks had their own part of

town, a cafe, a school, plenty of churches, and Ira's carpenter shop. Why couldn't they have a library? The black part of town slanted toward the swamps. Folks always kidded that someday the whole place might just slide right down into the muck. A swamp's no place for a library. Wouldn't be long before the books started growing Spanish moss. But those men had a point. What right did I have to decide what books folks could read and where they could read them?

"I won't tell anyone what or where they can read." I took a deep breath to keep from shaking. "I'm just going to build my library. You can all come if you like, or not. It's up to you."

I turned and started walking. Maybe I was a coward for leaving before they could talk back, but they kept right on talking even though I wasn't there to hear them. Sounded like a fight brewing to me, but I tried to keep my mind far enough away so I didn't hear it.

Back at home, I loaded up the wood-sided wagon I kept stored under the house. Armed with nails, a hammer, a ruler, paper, and a pencil, I figured myself prepared to do some shelf building. Wheeling over to the Carrolls', I gave a shout for Mary.

She ran right out. "Howdy, Nissa. Where you off to?"

"To build shelves in the library."

"You really going to do all that?"

"That's right. And you're going to help me unless you've got something better to do."

"Actually, Gary Journiette and I are going berry picking."

"You and Gary can berry pick any old time. This is something special."

"But Nissa . . ." Mary raced down her steps, then leaned in real close to me, whispering, "He's finally asked me to do something with him."

"Then ask him to do this with us."

Mary thought on it a minute. Calling over her shoulder, she said, "Ma, can I help Nissa build shelves for the library if Gary Journiette is there to pitch in?"

Mrs. Carroll leaned out Mary 's bedroom window, a sheet clutched in her hand. "Who else will be there?"

"Mr. Simmons will be coming out with a load of lumber," I told her.

Frowning, Mrs. Carroll said, "You keep your hands busy and your mind on work, Mary."

"Yes, ma'am."

"All right then. Good luck, Nissa."

Just as Mrs. Carroll stood up to go back inside, I shouted, "You have any books to donate?"

"I might when you've got the shelves built."

"Thank you, ma'am."

"Uh-huh." Mrs. Carroll disappeared into the darkness of the room.

Mary giggled. "I'm going to have a real bona fide date."

"Before you were planning on lying to your mama and meeting him in private?"

"That's right."

"Sounds treacherous to me," I said, dragging my wagon down the road. Mary took half a handle and off we went.

Taking a lay of the house once we got there, I found a new problem to solve. Each room had enough furniture in it to keep a family of four in style. Piling all that nice furniture up in a room would be like stuffing the spirit of a person into a box. On occasion when I walk into a house, I feel the person who lives there like a peaceful ghost. Packing away all that furniture would be like boxing up Lara.

Mary had gone off to scare up Gary Journiette, so I had time to sit on the front stoop and cogitate on the whole thing. The library'd have room for end tables, a few chairs, desks, and the bookcases Lara had, but that left plenty of furniture—more than our house in town could hold. Mama's room would need a few things, but that left rooms full of furniture.

"You'll get plenty of shelves built that way, Nissa Bergen." Gary Journiette stood in the front yard, his red hair sticking up like a scrub brush. Mary stood beside him grinning like she'd brought a prize pig to the fair.

"Let's see you build a shelf without wood."

Gary said, "I thought we were building shelves."

"When the wood gets here." I felt like knocking on his head to see if there was anything in it besides mushy old bits of brain that didn't work.

Turning to Mary, I asked, "What do you think we should do with all the furniture?"

"Oh, April and Winston would give up their baby for some furniture. They're living on things made out of the pallets Winston brings home from the feed store. April had to take a few of our kitchen chairs on account of the fact she's gotten so heavy, she breaks the pallet chairs every time she tries to sit on them."

Seeing April, wide as a hippopotamus, crashing to the floor made me wince and laugh at the same time. In my mind's eye, she looked like a strange kind of Goldilocks. "I'll have to see what Lara thinks of that. She might not want her furniture going out to people, but it sure beats sitting inside collecting moth holes."

Mary clapped her hands together. "April'll be happy enough to go into labor on the spot." We all laughed at that.

"Well, until the lumber gets here, we might as well push all the furniture away from the walls, so we can get the shelves in."

Gary said, "Moving furniture's a man's job."

"You want to move couches, beds, and dressers all by yourself, Gary?" That loud-mouthed boy didn't so much as come up to my shoulder.

"I could." He folded his arms over his chest.

"And end up springing your muscles loose like they were little more than spaghetti? I think not." I headed into the house. "You can protest if you want, Gary, but I'm moving furniture."

My comment wasn't too far off. By the time we had everything bunched up in the middle of each room, I felt like my entire body had been mushed like an overcooked noodle.

All three of us flopped down in the grass, huffing and puffing like a trio of plow horses that just dragged their way through a rocky field. After a bit of watching the clouds skitter by overhead, Mary asked, "Just who is going to work in this here library of yours, Nissa?"

"Me, for one."

"That's a given," Gary barked.

"And Lara." I decided to just ignore Gary's surly mood. "She thought she might like spending a little time in the old place."

Mary nudged me, saying, "She's having a baby."

"So's your sister, but she's hoping to put in an hour or two a week. I told both of them we could put a crib up next to the check-in desk. Come nap time, the two of them can bring the babies in for a snooze."

"Am I allowed to work in the library?" Mary asked.

"Sure thing. I won't turn anybody away who wants to help." Truth was a lot of folks volunteered to help out, from Rinnie Lee right down to Merle Thibodeaux.

"And me?" Gary piped in.

"You even know how to read?" I asked. Mary and I laughed.

"Shut your mouth, Nissa Bergen." Gary sat up. "I suppose

you're going to be that free with your books. If you are, folks'll probably just keep them."

"They can have them for a month. After that, they better bring them back or pay a fine."

"A fine?" Mary sat up.

"A penny a week," I announced. Actually, I'd made all that up on the spot. Before Gary started asking questions, I never even thought about borrowing rules.

"I'd like to see you try and collect a fine." Gary laughed.

About that time, Ira showed up with a load of wood.

After we unloaded all of the wood, Ira asked, "You want me to stick around and help the three of you out?"

"I'd be much obliged, Mr. Simmons," I told him.

"My mama always said, God handed me a hammer on my way out of heaven, so I figure I'm doing the Lord's work when I put one to good use."

The lumber stacked in the front yard, the four of us went to work. As the hours passed, the yard looked like it'd started to sprout bookshelves. The breed we'd sown would make most carpenters weep what with the warped boards and ugly old knots, some of which had holes in them big enough to let a silver dollar pass right through. Ira told me I built faster than a slave afraid of his master's whip. Gary and Mary turned out to be real good at holding things, but a little like clumsy bears when it came to planning out a set of shelves or actually hammering them together. That aside, we had four shelves up before Gary started complaining of an empty stomach.

Truth be told, I had a hankering for food, too. But that boy rubbed me the wrong way, so I told him he could just walk on home for his lunch if he was so hungry.

"Don't I even get a meal for all this work?"

"Why not go pick some berries," I told him.

"Now, Miss Nissa," Ira said. "Mr. Gary's been real good helping us out. He deserves something in return. I can drive us into the Gator. Rinnie Lee can serve us up something good."

Gary backed away a little. "I can't do that."

"Why not?" Mary asked.

I knew right off from the scared look in his eye. "Gary's afraid of other folks seeing him in the Gator."

"I am not!" Gary shouted.

Opening the door to Ira's truck, I said, "Then hop right on in."

Gary shook his head, saying, "Negro food's bad for you!"

"What?" Mary made a sour face that'd scare a spider from its web.

"Twists up your insides."

"Might give you a little gas, but that'll pass," I told Gary.

Ira put a hand over his mouth to hide his laughter. Clearing his throat, he said, "There's no need for fighting, children. I'll go into town and have Rinnie Lee pack up a picnic lunch."

"You sure?" Mary asked.

"Won't be much trouble."

As Ira drove off, Mary turned around and walloped Gary in the arm. "Gary Journiette, I should wash your eyes out with soap. You need to go color blind!"

"You see me building shelves with the man?" Gary shouted. "Didn't I pitch right in there? I don't have no quarrel with the coloreds, but if my daddy saw me driving around with one, I might as well shave my backside clean off before he even got to it."

Like me, Gary feared the punishment of bigots. Damn if that didn't seem lopsided enough to be a plan of the devil himself.

Ira came back with lunch, Lara, and Papa. Stepping out of the truck, Papa said, "We figured you could use some help."

"And I go where the food goes," Lara teased.

We laughed, then had ourselves a fine old picnic in the yard surrounded by bookshelves.

"These'll do real nice," Papa said, admiring our work.

"What do you think we ought to do with your furniture, Lara?"

"Burn it," Lara said, biting into a sandwich.

"Heavens," Mary gasped.

"She isn't serious." I leaned into Mary.

"Oh."

Lara laughed. "I don't know. We don't have room for it at the house."

"April and Winston can use some." Mary bowed her head in embarrassment. "Sorry to be so forward."

"That's all right, Mary. You're almost one of the family."

It still gave me a jiggle inside my heart when Lara said "family" and meant me, her, and Papa. I'm sure her idea of family didn't leave room for Mama.

"So," Lara rolled her eyes back in thought. "I suppose that'd mean giving some furniture to April and Winston would be keeping the furniture in the family."

"They'd take real good care of it, Lara," Mary promised.

"I'm sure they would."

Putting her sandwich down, Mary jumped to her feet. "Can I go tell them?"

"Now?" Lara asked, laughing.

"Yes, ma'am. They'll be thrilled."

Lara said, "All right, but stick a sandwich in your pocket. You need to eat."

Mary ran off shouting, "I'll be back!"

As I watched her hightail it down the road, I thought one day I'd have a little brother or sister who'd come running for me, telling me some big happy news. It made me feel the warmth of a hug that'd be years in the making.

"Look what I've done for you, Nissa." Papa handed me a scrap of newspaper. I could tell by the ink around the edges that it was a test piece for something Papa had a mind to add to the paper.

Taking it, I stared at an article about me. The title read, "Harper Resident Plans to Build Library." Papa went on for two columns about how his own daughter had designs on turning the Ross house into a library. At the end, he asked for donations of bookshelves and books, promising the new building would be a pleasurable addition to the town for all concerned. What it could be was a new battleground set to become kindling, but it sure felt good to see the story of my plan laid out on the page like that.

Kissing and hugging Papa, I said, "Thank you." Before I could even sit down again, I'd started to cry.

"Oh, Nissa," Lara looked like she'd start to cry, too, as she handed me her napkin, so I gave mine to her. Holding it in the air, she laughed through her tears.

The library felt right as we sat there on the grass. I believed it'd all work out in the end. How, I had no earthly clue, but I had faith. And that's plenty enough where plans are concerned.

A Sign

Turns out the grapevine did double as a delivery system. Papa's article gave my donations a boost, I'm sure. But they started coming in even before the article was printed. Seemed like folks in town had already decided how the library would be run. At the front door, I found stacks or boxes of books, left with notes, saying things like, "Donated by the Family of Mabel Carter for use by whites only." One such family even went so far as to paint "whites only" on the spines of the books. I felt like ripping the covers right off, but I painted over those ugly words instead.

At the back door, I found books wrapped in cheesecloth or left in stacks. Many of them had names signed in the covers. The notes left there said, "For your library, Miss Nissa" or "Here's something to fill your shelves."

Some folks even left bookshelves on the grass. Many of the donors left other little things like blueberry muffins, oatmeal cookies with currants, or a thank-you note telling me how happy they were to have a library going up in town. As the books started filling up the rooms, we brought the furniture out, a whole truckload of it going to April and Winston, and the rest to a storage room in Ira Simmons's shop to wait on Lara's decision of what to do with it. April and Winston couldn't stop thanking Lara for the furniture. Winston's mouth went faster than a jackrabbit trying to keep ahead of a forest fire all the while he helped Papa, Mr. Carroll, and Ira unload the truck. April just stood around looking like a spooked deer, saying, "I can't believe this is all ours."

The polished, fancy furniture looked like a male peacock in a henhouse in that little old clapboard place they lived in. As they put the bed together, I thought how nice it would be for April to bring her child into the world on a real bed instead of the beat-up old mattress they'd been using. No number of blankets would make that kind of bed feel soft.

Of course, we kept enough furniture to give Mama a room. Lara even liked the idea. She said it'd give Mama her independence when she was in town. I figured that also meant giving herself a degree of freedom.

Even some of the kids at school started handing me library donations. They didn't needle me for stories about Mama. For the first time in my life, folks talked more about what I was doing right than what my mama was doing wrong.

As I left school the first day with a stack of books, I decided to cut across the Journiette fields to go straight to the library. Coming out across from Peter Robidoux's house, I kept my eyes on the road for fear he'd see me and use the opportunity to give me yet another piece of his crazy mind.

Sure enough, he came running after me, shouting, "Hold up, Nissa."

Turning, I saw that he had a book in his hand. "What's that?"

Stopping to catch his breath, Peter said, "A copy of *Treasure Island* my grandpa gave me."

"You're donating it?"

"All the kids in school donated something."

As usual, Peter had a slanted view on how things really happened. Only five kids at school donated anything, but that meant five more books for the library. "That book's special, Peter. Maybe you should keep it."

"I'm donating it!" Peter shoved the book in my face.

"All right then, put it on the top." I held out the stack in my arms. He dropped his book on it.

"Will my name go on a plaque somewhere?"

"A plaque?"

"Yeah, Aunt Chessie says people who donate things get remembered by having their names on plaques."

So that was his motive. "Well, I don't have any money for a plaque, Peter. Is your name in the book?"

"Sure."

"Then everyone who reads it's going to know you donated it."

Peter smiled. "I'd like that." Don't know why, but something told me that the smile on his face wasn't one of smug pride. He actually felt good about giving people a book to read.

"Thank you, Peter. I'm sure folks'll appreciate it. I know I love following Jim Hawkins across the ocean."

"You like that book?"

"Sure."

"It's a book about boys."

"So? I don't figure there's anything Jim did in that book I couldn't do."

Peter shook his head. "Knowing you, Nissa, you're right." He walked away muttering to himself. That boy sure was a puzzlement. I'd never figure him out.

As the weeks ticked by, my library grew shelf by shelf. Didn't seem like anything could stop it. Even the death of Huey Long didn't put but a small dent into the stream of donations. He was killed in the early part of September. A lot of folks took to whispering and fretting over what would come of Louisiana now that the Kingfish was dead. Mama wrote and put confetti in the envelope to celebrate the end of what she called the "Louisiana dictatorship." Still, being shot was no way for a man to die. Even Mama agreed to that. We all said our good-byes at a special church service. A few people even gave me books afterward, saying they'd donated them in the name of Huey Long, who wanted to see all of Louisiana's children with books in their hands. I doubted that, knowing how Mr. Long felt about black folks, but I smiled just the same.

Seeing the library grow made me happy enough to wake up laughing after a night of good dreams, but I still hadn't received anything I'd care to call a message from above. Then one day, I was out front weeding the flower beds when a car came chugging up. I thought it'd just drive on by into town, like the other cars that'd passed by that day, but it stopped square in front of the door.

An old man stepped out wearing a suit the likes of those I'd seen in Chicago. Walking around the front of the car, he said, "Are you Miss Bergen?"

Used to people calling Mama that, I had to think twice before answering, "Yes, sir."

"Well then, I have a delivery for you." Opening the back door of his coachlike car, he let me see the piles of boxes, each one filled to the rim with books.

"Heavens." Just saying Gods address told me what was headed my way.

"I taught down in New Orleans for thirty-five years. Now it's time for someone else to benefit from my library. I feel kind of selfish sitting on all these books."

"You drove all the way up here from New Orleans?"

"Yes, ma'am."

I knew a godsend when I saw one, but curiosity ran my tongue. "How'd you hear about my library?"

"Vernon Finch was a student of mine years back. He told me about your plans."

"I can't begin to thank you."

"Having all these books read will be thanks enough."

That old man and I carried books for over an hour. I thanked God for sending such a man my way with each box I brought into the house. We both looked like we'd taken a shower in sweat by the time we'd emptied his car. I offered him a glass of lemonade. Standing in the kitchen, I couldn't help wondering if an angel didn't whisper in that man's ear to send him all that way. As he handed me the glass back, saying, "Thank you, Miss Bergen," I realized I didn't know his name.

"Sir," I said as I followed him to the front room.

"Yes?" He turned to face me, hat in hand.

"What's your name?"

"Dr. Archibald Lestor."

"Thank you, Dr. Lestor." I held out my hand.

He shook it, smiling. "Thank you, Miss Bergen. You take good care of my books, now."

I will.

"I'll be by once you've finished the place, so send word to Vernon for me." He stepped outside.

"Don't you want to stay over in Harper? You've got a long drive ahead."

"No ma'am. I've got a sister just down the road a piece."

And like that, he was gone, leaving me with a room full of books. I walked over to the tallest pile and there on the top sat a book called *Separate But Equal*. Mrs. Owens taught us all about the fact that Louisiana passed a law making blacks and whites travel in different train cars and a long while back it became a national law when the Supreme Court told old Homer Plessy he had no right to ride in a white man's car as long as whites and blacks remained separate, but equal.

Trouble was most white folks used faulty weights when they measured out equality. Black cars on the train had bare wooden benches and no food services except for the sandwich boys who rarely had anything left by the time they got to the back of the train. And Harper was one great example of Louisiana equality with the black folks living in a swamp.

Still, I took that book as my sign. I'd take those Supreme Court judges at their word, but this time the scales would be even. Cutting the house right down the middle, the two sides would be totally equal. I'd divide my book collection right down the middle. I'd let the white people go on thinking they had the better deal by using the front door and all, but the house would be divided into the East Harper Library and the West Harper Library. There'd be no WHITES ONLY sign on my walls.

Now, in a world where color doesn't matter, my solution wasn't right. But if Mama had taught me anything, it was that in this here world there's no such thing as living a righteous life. Only Jesus could do that. Me, I was going to do the best I could. And that meant two libraries in the same building, each one as good as the other. Besides, who wanted to spend their reading time with bigoty old white people anyhow?

Using Mama's bedroom, which fell on the west side of the house, I painted up signs. Painting made me think of Mama. Her letters came as regular as cricket songs after I got back to Harper. Almost every day, there was a letter stuck into the frame of our screen door. Papa stopped at the post office each morning before going to work so he could keep Chessie Roubidoux's gossipy fingers off my Mama's letters. She didn't even have the mail bag open when Papa showed up on most mornings.

Each letter was like a cartoon of Mama's life. In almost every paragraph, Mama drew me a little picture of what she was talking about—the play set, the painting she put on her studio wall, the couch she got for her parlor, and the rosebushes in her roof garden. I felt close enough to hear her laugh just by reading those letters.

As my signs dried, I wrote Mama a letter telling her all that had happened and how my library became two. I even took a stab at drawing her room. It looked more like a coffee stain than a picture, but it would do. I didn't inherit one bit of Mama's drawing talent, but I knew my sketch would make her smile.

On every door that closed off one library from the other, I put up signs which said, THIS WAY TO THE EAST HARPER LIBRARY, EVERYONE WELCOME. Substituting "West" for "East," the other side said the same thing. I knew nobody would step through those doors, but I had to show folks what I really wanted in a public library.

I had a hammer in hand to put up the last sign when Mary came charging through the front door, shouting, "The babies are coming!"

Sounding like Paul Revere, Mary looked as if she was being chased by the British, all nervous and sweaty. "What do you mean babies? Is April having twins?"

"No," Mary shook her head like she hoped it'd come off. "Lara's having pains, too."

"Lara?" I dropped the hammer. "Her baby isn't due until after Halloween."

Bennie had been born early. I knew what that meant.

"Well, she's pacing the floor with cramps so bad they can only be one thing. And April's already screaming about hers."

"All right." Instantly, my insides felt like they'd been fed into a coal chute. My stomach dropping, my heart spinning, I thought I'd pass out. "You go to April, I'll go to Lara."

Mary and I never ran so hard in our lives. April screamed loud enough to be heard at the end of Main Street. Folks milled around on the mercantile porch waiting for news. The Carroll house was filled with people. As I ran in our front door, I saw Papa and Lara walking together. He held her around the waist as if to hold her up, and she had a tight grip on both of his hands. Lara's breathing was real heavy and mixed with tiny cries of pain. Seeing me, she said, "Nissa!" like I'd come back from the dead. "I'm so glad you're here."

"Is Dr. Swenson coming?"

"He's with April now."

"What about Lara? Her baby's early."

Swallowing her pain, Lara said, "Rinnie Lee's coming. She's delivered plenty of babies."

"But it's early!"

"Nissa, calm down," Papa said, but I could almost hear his pulse galloping along. His eyes were wild with worry. "Everything's going to be all right."

Spending all my time at the library, I barely ever thought about the baby. I should have been praying for the baby's health all along. I tried cramming a month's worth of prayer into that one day. I had a prayer going in my head at all times, even while I brought Lara cool water to drink, pillows, or ice to suck. Rinnie Lee showed up and the three of us helped Lara to the old keeping room.

I'd never heard a woman swear that much, not even when Mama slammed her finger in the car door. When Lara began yelling, I started pacing the hall, praying out loud. Dr. Swenson kept stopping by to see how Lara was getting along, then disappearing to go check in on April.

Lara would get quiet for a bit, then scream. She pulled on my nerves like they were a yo-yo. I prayed louder. I was nearly yelling when the baby let out a newborn cry. Thanking the Lord, I ran in there.

Covered in blood, the baby looked like a pulpy peach pit, all wrinkled and tiny. "Is it all right?"

"She's fine," Rinnie Lee whispered.

"A baby girl." I laughed through tears. I wanted to touch her, but Lara seemed to be resting in an earthbound corner of heaven at that moment, her eyes reveling at the sight of her baby girl. Papa stood over her, looking as proud as Joseph. Then Lara got pains again. What most folks don't talk about is that after the baby comes out, the mama has to deliver the little sack the baby lived in for nine months. Or for eight in my sister's case.

Papa took the baby to clean her off while Rinnie Lee helped Lara through the last bit of labor. I joined Papa in the kitchen as he used warm water to wash the baby who cried like he'd used sandpaper instead of a towel. "She's hungry."

"And scared, I imagine." Going from a warm, dark place to a drafty, bright kitchen couldn't be a desirable change. The thought of getting cold made me remember the quilt. Rushing upstairs, I came back just as Papa finished drying her off.

"Happy birthday, baby girl," I said, as I wrapped her in the quilt.

Rinnie Lee went off to bury the afterbirth, so it was just us four when Papa brought the baby to Lara for her first meal. Touching her silky head, I realized my little sister had found a way to tug at my soul. I felt little charges of happiness all through me. "What's her name?"

"Lily Maeve," Papa said, smiling as he rubbed her tiny little knuckles.

"That's real nice." Brushing Lily's cheek, I thought of rose petals and how much I wished it was Mama in that bed holding her baby. But that didn't come to pass, so I prayed God would make Mama as happy as Lara was at that moment in His own way.

Dr. Swenson came by thinking he'd help bring Lily into the world, but he gave her an examination instead. Handing the baby back to her mama, he said, "She looks strong and healthy, Lara. You keep her warm and well-fed and this little girl will be terrorizing Harper in no time."

Lara laughed. Papa shook Dr. Swenson s hand and started laughing like a schoolboy. As he walked Dr. Swenson to the door, Papa kept asking questions like, "Do her lungs sound clear? How often should we check on her at night?"

Dr. Swenson stopped, put his hands on Papas shoulders, then said, "She's healthy, Ivar. Put your worries to bed."

Papa nodded, tears streaming down his face. We all knew he feared Lily might fall prey to the same illness that took Bennie. But, already, Lily looked redder and healthier than Bennie ever did.

April didn't bring her son, Franklin Lawford Caveat, into the world until after midnight. That poor girl had to work long and hard for her miracle. That night as I lay in bed, I couldn't help thinking how another Bergen and Carroll (once removed) would be growing up together, probably as best friends. I fell asleep feeling that the world had settled a little bit more evenly that night.

Growing

In my mind, Lily and the libraries share a birthday. I prayed they'd grow together, too. In the beginning they sure did. As Lily gained weight, learned to smile, and started kicking her feet, Ira and I carved signs for the East and West yards and Mary and I dug up a path to the West door. Papa helped me lay down the stepping-stones we took out of the Journiette field rock pile.

Mama and I feverishly exchanged letters during all that time. And I invited her to the opening of the libraries so we could celebrate together. She'd even be able to stay on through Halloween, her second-favorite holiday. Mama promised to arrive on opening day and I believed her. Mama and I had grown, too—closer together and farther apart in all the ways that matter.

And me, well, I guess growing up wasn't all that awful after all. The problems did get harder, but not without me getting a little wiser—that is, if I kept my head about me and my heart full of prayers. In those days, most of my prayers focused on Lily staying healthy and the town taking to the idea of two libraries in one.

Folks started coming out almost every day to see how the library was progressing. They pointed and gossiped, asked questions, and gave their own answers when they didn't like mine. Some folks even helped write out the cards for the catalogue we'd keep in the old apothecary drawers the Minkies donated.

Chessie said she'd start a reading circle. Mrs. Linzy asked if she could host a Bible Study on Wednesday night. I agreed to the ideas with pleasure, not that I really wanted to hear what those ladies had to say about the Bible or any other book. I just knew that was their way of saying they liked the East Library.

And the West Library had plenty of visitors, too. The Villeneuves brought in their books. Ira and Rinnie Lee came to create built-in shelves for the children's room. Everyone in town knew the two of them would get married someday, so I figured they had plans of bringing somebody of their own around to use that room in a few years.

Mary and I put together the children's room for the East Library with April supervising. I told anybody who'd listen how I planned to have Mama paint characters all over the walls of the children's rooms. And those paintings did appear in time—Winnie-the-Pooh marched through the Hundred Acre Wood of the East Library with all his friends. And Brer Rabbit joined Little Eight John, John Henry, and High John de Conqueror in the West Library.

Mama kept her promise and then some. She arrived by train a week before opening day. Running down the steps, she dropped her suitcase, then said, "Let me see that baby girl!" Lara held Lily out, the sun quilt dangling around her. Mama scooped Lily up in a flash. "Aren't you the prize of heaven on earth." She rubbed the baby's chin and made her gurgle. Some folks say babies coo, but I reckon those folks haven't heard a pigeon. Babies' voices don't have the smooth rhythm of a coo. Their voices bounce and dribble because its a brand new toy they're playing with there.

Handing the baby back, Mama said, "That quilt sure did come out mighty nice." Then she leaned forward and actually gave Lara a kiss, saying, "Congratulations, Lara."

Lara blushed, saying, "Thank you, Heirah Rae."

Mama whirled around to face me. "How do, Miss Librarian." Mama picked me up and squeezed me until my eyes nearly ended up on her shoulder. "I'm so proud of you."

"Thanks, Mama."

"Show me this library." Mama looped her arm in mine. "I want the grand tour."

"It's libraries, Mama. East and West."

"I'm holding on to hope, Nissa. It'll be one library in time, I wager." She winked.

Mama loved every bit of it, especially the paint I put over the "whites only" books. The first thing she did when she got to her room was take out her paints. "I'll bring these walls alive."

"I'd love that, Mama."

The libraries grew by rooms, fields, and other natural wonders. Mama painted Grower's Meadow on the old dining room wall. Sutton's Creek flowed between two shelves in the East Library. The woods out past the mercantile extended the entry wall of the West Library. Mama'd brought the world of Harper inside. Painting night and day, I thought Mama would work herself into a stupor, but all that painting just made her happier. She whistled, sang, and even danced her way through that week.

As I travelled through the rooms the night before the opening, I noticed something I hadn't before. Mama had changed her murals. Now, Mary and I splashed each other in Sutton's Creek. Papa and Lara walked with a toddling baby between them in Grower's Meadow. And Mama'd added a new mural on the landing of the front stairs. Walking up, I came face to face with myself, smiling like I'd just won a blue ribbon. Hugged on one side by Mama and by Papa on the other, we looked like a happy family once again. Of course, now Lara stood shoulder to shoulder with Papa, baby Lily in her arms.

When I got home, Papa came into my room. I didn't even dream of sleeping. I sat on a windowsill watching the rain fall on the garden. He sat beside me, a gift in his lap.

"This is from Lara and me." He handed it over.

Inside the wrapping there were two boxes. In the top box, I found a leather-bound book filled with thick black lines. A ribbon ran down the center page, and a heavy fountain pen fit into a leather pocket on the front cover.

"It's so all your guests can sign in." Papa tapped the other box. "One for each library."

"Thank you, Papa." I hugged him.

Smiling as a tear slid onto his check, he said, "No, Nissa, thank you."

"For what?"

"Being happy. That's a father's greatest joy—to see his children happy."

It sure made me feel good to hear him say "children." And he was right. I felt happy-more content and glad to be alive than I'd felt in years. I guess the whole family had grown into the people they'd always wanted to be. Hugging the books, I said, "Thank you."

Kissing me on the forehead, he said, "You're welcome."

"Tell Lara thanks," I said as he left.

The next morning, I couldn't decide where I should be—in the East Harper Library or the West Harper Library. I wanted to be with all my friends on the west side, but the other folks in town would put up a fuss, so I snuck from one side to the other through a closet in what used to be an upstairs bedroom. We had two picnics going on either side of the building. Everyone brought a dish to pass. Folks wandered through the shelves, looking at books, talking, and marveling at Mama's murals.

I even overheard Mrs. Linzy say, "I hate to say it, but that woman paints with the hand of God."

Heading down the east stairs, I met Papa coming in the front door. "Nissa, you've got to come see who's here."

I figured it would be Dr. Lestor come to see how his books looked on the shelves, but stepping outside I got hit with a wind of surprise. Grandma Dee and Grandpa Jared stood at the edge of the road amongst the crowd.

"Grandma! Grandpa!" I shouted, running across the lawn.

They both drew me up in a hug. Grandpa Jared said, "Your mama made sure we came."

"I'm so glad you're here!"

"We would've been here sooner, but the car broke down." Grandma Dee looked like she wanted to cry. "I made you a dress to wear today." She handed me the wrapped package.

"I'll put it on right now!" I ran straight inside.

Stopping in the upstairs hallway, I could see out over to the West Library picnic. Otis Dupree had come with his band. They had people tearing up the grass with their jiggety beat. People laughed, kids ran, and the food kept coming as more folks arrived.

I passed through a doorway into the East Library knowing I was one of only a few people who dared walk through. It gave me a chill. I thanked God for my life and the libraries. Staring at the door I came through, I hoped Mama was right—that some-day folks would walk through that door going in both directions. Heading down the stairs, I actually believed I could wait for it to happen.

Standing in a front room, I could see the folks below. A few of them shook their heads and leaned in close to gossip—over Mr. Dupree's band, I supposed. Most folks seemed happy enough enjoying their picnic or sitting under a tree to read a book. Gary and Mary sat on the bench beside the rose garden, chatting away like two crows on a fence. Lara and April shared a blanket with the babies. Papa sat between them entertaining the little ones with a rattle. Mama walked through the garden with her parents. I hoped she was telling them about Chicago and convincing them they should go up for a visit.

Going into Mama's room, I closed the door to open the dress box. Blue as a deep lake on a clear day, the dress didn't stop at my knees, it went down to midcalf in loose folds. Turning, I saw that it was a woman's dress with a wide sailor's collar and a nice, gauzy sash around the waist. Tying it on, I felt right pretty. I still looked like a girl in a woman's dress, but I figured I'd grow into it.

Walking downstairs, I stopped on the landing to put my hand on Mama's mural, knowing I was in my own place.

Alexandria LaFaye jokes, "If breathing wasn't automatic, I'd die. I'm terrible at doing anything routinely." She often wonders how her artistic ways might affect others, especially her daughter, Adia. That question inspired her to create Heirah Rae, Nissa Bergen's free-spirited mama.

After finishing *The Year of the Sawdust Man*, Alexandria wanted to give Nissa the same self-awareness and independence that Heirah Rae acquired in the first book. Nissa struggled to learn how to live her daily life without her mother, but she needed to take that extra step and learn to live for herself and not just her mother. In *Nissa's Place*, she does just that.

As a child, libraries were one of Alexandria's favorite places to spend time. She still enjoys her treks to the library, but now, as a teach of creative writing in the low-residency MFA programs at Hamline and Hollins, she's helping other people fill future libraries with their own writing. If you'd like to check out Alexandria's place on the web, please visit www.alafaye.com.

I'm grateful to Milkweed Editions for giving Nissa a place on their list. Ben, Jessica, and the rest of the folks at Milkweed have done a stellar job with the "whole package" of bringing a book to print and sharing it with readers. Thank you all! And I'll be forever thankful for God's guidance as I write.

More Books from Milkweed Editions

If you enjoyed this book, you'll also want to read
these other Milkweed novels.
To order books or for more information, contact Milkweed at
(800) 520-6455
or visit our Web site (www.milkweed.org).

The Year of the Sawdust Man
A. LaFaye

Water Steps
A. LaFaye

The Keening
A. LaFaye

The Linden Tree
Ellie Mathews

Remember As You Pass Me By
L. King Pérez

Milkweed Editions

Founded in 1979, Milkweed Editions is one of the largest independent, nonprofit literary publishers in the United States. Milkweed publishes with the intention of making a humane impact on society, in the belief that good writing can transform the human heart and spirit.

Join Us

Milkweed depends on the generosity of foundations and individuals like you, in addition to the sales of its books. In an increasingly consolidated and bottom-line-driven publishing world, your support allows us to select and publish books on the basis of their literary quality and the depth of their message. Please visit our Web site (www.milkweed.org) or contact us at (800) 520-6455 to learn more about our donor program.

Milkweed Editions, a nonprofit publisher, gratefully acknowledges sustaining support from Emilie and Henry Buchwald; the Patrick and Aimee Butler Foundation; the Dougherty Family Foundation; the Ecolab Foundation; the General Mills Foundation; John and Joanne Gordon; William and Jeanne Grandy; the Jerome Foundation; Robert and Stephanie Karon; the Lerner Foundation; Sally Macut; Sanders and Tasha Marvin; the McKnight Foundation; Mid-Continent Engineering; the Minnesota State Arts Board, through an appropriation by the Minnesota State Legislature, a grant from the Wells Fargo Foundation Minnesota, and a grant from the National Endowment for the Arts; Kelly Morrison and John Willoughby; the National Endowment for the Arts, and the American Reinvestment and Recovery Act; the Navarre Corporation; Ann and Doug Ness; Jörg and Angie Pierach; the RBC Foundation USA; Ellen Sturgis; the Target Foundation; the James R. Thorpe Foundation; the Travelers Foundation; Moira and John Turner; and Edward and Jenny Wahl.

MINNESOTA
STATE ARTS BOARD

NATIONAL
ENDOWMENT
FOR THE ARTS
A great nation
deserves great art.

TARGET.

THE McKNIGHT FOUNDATION

Interior design by Connie Kuhnz
Typeset in Berkeley Oldstyle by BookMobile Design
and Publishing Services
Printed on acid-free Natures Recycled paper
by Versa Press